MACKINAC PASSAGE: A SUMMER ADVENTURE

Robert A. Lytle
Illustrated by Karen Howell

Thunder Bay Press

Holt, Michigan

Mackinac Passage: A Summer Adventure
© 1995 by Robert Lytle

Printed in the United States of America

04 03 02 01 00   4 3

ISBN 1-882376-11-0

Cover and text illustrations by Karen Howell

Thunder Bay Press
P.O. Box 580
Holt, Michigan 48842

Dedicated to my mom and dad.

Car ferry, Straits of Mackinac

CHAPTER 1
THE FIRST SIGN

Friday, June 13 11:00 a.m.

Howard Jenkins pulled the blue 1949 Ford off the highway into the Texaco station at Grayling.

"Wake up, kids," Averill Jenkins called. "We won't be stopping again until we get to the Straits."

Pete was sweltering between two suitcases and a box of kitchen utensils. His older sister, Cara, was sleeping comfortably on the other side of the back seat with her head on a pillow and her window open.

As they stepped out of the car and stretched their legs, the gas station owner raced past them shouting at the back end of a new 1952 Cadillac pulling out and heading south. He stood along the shoulder of U.S. 27, frantically waving his arms.

"Hey! Come back here!" he yelled.

Pete's dad had opened the hood while his mom was unwrapping some sandwiches. They all stared as Mr. Byers stalked back to his office.

"That's the fifth one this month," he muttered as he passed Mr. Jenkins.

1

Pete and Cara went in to use the restrooms while Pete's dad checked the trailer hitch that pulled the Jenkins' new boat. As Pete was walking out of the bathroom, Harry Byers was standing by his cash register yelling into the telephone.

"Of course, I'm sure," he screamed. "It's got the same number as the other four. . . . Yes, I'm positive. They've all been from tourists heading south on 27. No, I learned my lesson not to deposit it, but you guys gotta do something. I'm going broke. . . . Yeah, I'll hold it here."

He slammed the receiver down and thumbtacked the fake bill to a cork board.

Cara came out of the restroom. "Let's go, Pete."

"Just a sec, Cara. Check this. It's a fake twenty."

Cara studied the bill closely. "No, look, it can't be. See these tiny red and blue hairs? Counterfeiters can't make paper like that. I learned it in Civics. Come on. Dad's waving for us."

They rushed out of the gas station and piled into the back seat. Mrs. Jenkins offered them a peanut butter and jelly or liver sausage sandwich, hardly a choice as far as Pete was concerned. He munched his PB & J as they whizzed along U.S. 27. Burma Shave ads popped up about every twenty miles. The one north of Gaylord read,

> *The big new tube*
> *Is like Louise,*
> *You get a thrill*
> *From every squeeze!*
> *BURMA SHAVE*

The six hour drive from the Jenkins' home in Saginaw north to their cottage in the Les Cheneaux

Islands was always long, hot, and tedious, but this year Pete didn't mind. He had just graduated from ninth grade into high school, and more importantly, Cara had finished high school and soon would be going away to college. Pete was quietly jubilant that he would finally be rid of his life-long nemesis.

The only interesting part the rest of the way came at the Straits of Mackinac. At the northern tip of lower Michigan, U.S. 27 opened into a giant parking lot for cars waiting to cross into the upper peninsula. After two hours of stopping and starting, Pete's dad eventually drove up to the edge of the dock and into the gaping maw of the monstrous ship, its gangplank surging four feet with the waves. The Ford clanked loudly twice on the loading ramp and then rolled deep into the dark, cavernous hold of the *Cheboygan* and was crammed into place with 150 other cars.

Pete raced up the metal stairs to the top deck and gazed out over the railing at the yachts heading to and from Mackinac Island. Across the short stretch of water was the grandest of all summer resorts. Pete stood transfixed by the vision of the Grand Hotel and the smaller summer homes along the west bluff. He would give anything to go there, even for a day. But he knew how expensive it was. Besides, he didn't want to waste time away from his own cottage, either.

After the ferry landed in St. Ignace Pete went back to his car and fell asleep until his mother awakened him again. "We're almost there," she said as they rolled past the Standard Oil station. Soon all the sights, smells, and sounds of Cedarville, the Hub of the Snows, made Pete sit up in anticipation. The Ford turned onto Hodeck Street as kids were scurrying across the dusty road to the Cedar Inn. Some carried long stringers of fish. Others, with red coffee cans in their hands and bamboo poles cradled across their shoulders raced toward the bay. The Jenkins coasted by the Bon Air and Hossack's General Store before stopping at the Cedarville Post Office.

Pete waited as his mom and dad went in to inform Mr. Visnaw, the postmaster, that they had arrived for the summer. As they approached the door, an old man carrying two large boxes blustered past them practically knocking Pete's mom into the street. She stepped aside and watched him as he barged along his way.

"I'll be right back," Pete said to Cara. He rolled into the front seat, opened the door, and ran past the old man all the way to the Bon Air.

Just as Cedarville was the hub of the Snows, the Bon Air was the hub of Cedarville. Pete pulled the screen door open and rushed in. The soda fountain, the candy counter, and the souvenirs were all there. The little shop was jammed with resorters standing in the aisles or seated at the tables. Pete could barely hear the juke box over the din of spoons clinking, cash registers ringing, and everybody chattering and laughing at once.

Then Pete noticed Mrs. Clark, the owner, talking angrily on the telephone. After she'd hung up, she showed a crisp, twenty dollar bill to Jack Frazier, the soda jerk. Her frown deepened when he shook his head and shrugged his shoulders. She turned and tacked the bill on the wall with two others.

Pete pushed his way back through the door and jogged along the sidewalk past Hossack's. He followed the wide road out to the end of the municipal dock where several kids were casting their fishing lines. He looked across the bay where, two miles down the channel, his cottage sat high on a bluff.

Pete's end of Big LaSalle Island had no electricity. No radios, telephones, or running water. Even the clocks ran slow. The Elliot Row cottagers' only communication with the rest of the world was by boat. Pete fished and swam and hiked every day of the summer. As fancy a place as Mackinac Island must be, he couldn't believe it was any better than right here in the Snows. As he looked out over Cedarville Bay, not one cloud intruded into his hemisphere.

"Petey-wetey," came a call from the head of the dock.

Well, perhaps one. Whenever Cara wanted to get Pete's attention and his goat at the same time, she knew that yelling "Petey-wetey" would result in immediate success. She reserved it for occasions when Pete was near people other than her parents, and she was out of his reach. Cara was a master of the taunt and her technique was flawless.

"Dad wants you to come right now."

Pete turned and ran back to the car to help put the two boats into the water.

The previous fall Mr. Jenkins bought a wooden, 15-foot runabout and outfitted it with an 18-horsepower, Hiawatha motor. The boat wasn't new; in fact, it was pretty old, but Pete and his dad had spent every weekend that winter fiberglassing the hull. They installed a steering wheel, dashboard, and a Plexiglas windshield. They built new seats and varnished the inside. By the end of spring she looked pretty good.

Pete's dad decided to keep the little aluminum boat, the *Tiny Tin*, as they now called it, for fishing and use the wooden boat, the *Flossy*, for the daily trip to town and for special excursions.

With any more than two aboard, the *Tiny Tin* could go no faster than a crawl so none of the Jenkins had ever bothered to venture any farther than their own bay. Now, with the *Flossy*, all thirty of the Les Cheneaux, or "Snows" islands would be within Pete's reach.

The Jenkins unloaded the car, filled the two outboards, and inched their way out into Cedarville Bay to the channel. They chugged along the shore of Cincinnati Row with all of its sturdy boathouses and luxurious summer homes nestled behind the dense grove of cedar trees that lined the beach.

Finally the two small boats came out of the channel and into a wide bay. They rounded the Elliot Hotel pier and Pete could see the old hotel and the small Elliot Row cabins that sat high on the bluff. They tied their boats to the narrow, wood plank dock and carried all the boxes and suitcases up the steep hill to the porch, and then inside to the musty air and creaky floors of their old, two bedroom cabin.

CHAPTER 2
TALKING FISH

Friday, June 13 3:00 p.m.

With everything lugged up from shore, all Pete had were a few cottage-opening duties and he'd be free for the summer. It was hot enough to strip off his tee-shirt and he got started. First, he unlocked and swept the outhouse. Then he and his dad set up the rain water catch tank by the back porch. Next, they each pumped and carried home ten pails of water from the community well down the path and poured them into the tank. Hopefully that would be enough for a few days until a good rain could fill it.

Then they helped finish the inside chores. With the beds made and the floors swept, Pete took a break and stretched out on the living room sofa. He thumbed idly through the large basket of old photographs and post cards. The people sure dressed funny in the olden days when his mom was a girl. But the thing he couldn't believe was all the fancy picnics and boating trips they had back then. Each picture showed twenty or thirty men, women, and children all duded up in their Sunday best. Even the fishing pictures. Pete closed his eyes and tried to imagine what it was like when his mom was young and the cottage was new.

———

"Wake up, Pete. Dinner's almost ready," she called in from the kitchen. "You can help your dad clean the two bass he just caught off the Davis' dock."

"No kidding, Ma, really? Two bass?"

Pete rolled off the sofa scattering the photographs as he scrambled to his feet. He raced out through the kitchen pushing the back screen door up against the wash stand and dashed past the outhouse to the fish-cleaning station. His dad was just taking two largemouths off his chain stringer.

"Wow! They must be five pounds each! What'd you get 'em on?" Pete asked.

"What? These?" his dad began slowly. "You mean these fish? Oh, I didn't catch them. No. It was the darnedest thing, Pete. They just followed me home."

Fishing secrets were sacred. Neither Pete nor his dad ever offered one without first striking some sort of bargain.

"Nope, you probably won't believe this, Pete, but I was just down at the Flowers' boathouse, didn't even take my rod and reel. As I turned to come home, these two bass jumped right out of the water and said, `Oh, please, mister, we're so hungry. Won't you take us home for dinner?' `Well,' I told them, `it would be my pleasure.' So, here they are."

"Come on, what'd you get 'em on?"

"All right. You scale 'em, and I'll tell you. Deal?"

"Deal."

There may have been fancier times and more elegant places, but there was never a better fish dinner than the one in the Jenkins' kitchen that night.

CHAPTER 3
THE BIG ONE

Saturday, June 14 8:30 a.m.

"Pete," Mr. Jenkins whispered the next morning as he nudged his son's shoulder. "Wake up."

Pete slowly opened his eyes to find a large, grayish figure next to his bed. Half asleep, Pete pulled the quilt over his head. Gradually, he noticed a clanking sound right in front of his nose and it suddenly dawned on him what was making all the racket. He pulled down the blanket and found two northern pike dancing at the end of his dad's chain stringer.

"Whoa!" Pete sat up bumping his head on the upper bunk springs. These were monsters. Each had to be over thirty inches long.

"I tried to get you up earlier, Pete," Mr. Jenkins continued. "Come on, they've just started hitting. I caught these less than fifteen minutes ago."

Pete scrambled into his blue jeans and sweatshirt and dashed through the curtain into the living room.

"Wear a warm hat and coat, Pete. I'll get your cushion and pole and start down to the boat."

Pete tied his shoes and grabbed an old, wool coat that had belonged to Grandma Heidelberg who had owned the cabin before willing it to Pete's mother. She had died two years before Pete was even born but her coat lived courageously on.

From the hat rack, Pete grabbed his captain's cap and quietly slipped out the front door.

He pulled the collar up over his ears as he dashed down the winding stone path to the dock.

"Where'd you catch 'em?" Pete asked as he hopped from the narrow dock into the bow of the aluminum boat. Even in the lee of the stone crib the waves bounced the *Tiny Tin* around like a rubber duck in a bath tub.

"Just past the Islington Hotel dock. The waves aren't too bad on the mainland side of the channel," his dad said as he pulled the starter cord on the five horsepower, Chris-Craft motor. "Hold on, here we go."

Howard Jenkins pointed the nose of the boat around the end of the dock and ran smack into the first wave. Pete bounced on the cushion and grabbed his pole to keep it from flying overboard. It was a slow, bumpy, one mile ride to Islington Point, and when Pete glanced around, he noticed that theirs was the only boat on the water. As the engine idled down to trolling speed, Pete cast his silver Dardevle out thirty feet to starboard.

"Here's where I got the second one, Pete," Howard Jenkins said as he tossed his lure almost onto the end of the Islington Hotel dock. "Right there."

Pete settled back in his seat and watched the activity three hundred yards across the channel in front of Cincinnati Row. Along that shore, he had always been aware of dozens of kids his age who were tantalizingly close, geographically, but light years beyond his reach, socially and financially.

Besides, they were always too preoccupied with their own friends and activities to ever notice him. He remembered what his mom had said about Cincinnati Row. It was named because, at about the turn of the century, many of the wealthy families of southern Ohio chose this stretch of Big LaSalle Island to build their summer homes. They brought with them their families, friends, and traditions and constructed fabulous lodges, complete with electricity, running water, refrigerators, and telephones. They brought staffs of servants to help throughout the summer. Each family had their own boathouse that sheltered sleek mahogany speedboats, luxurious cabin-cruisers, graceful sailboats and powerful outboards.

The Elliot Hotel, along with Pete's cottage and ten or eleven other small cabins of Elliot Row, were separated from Cincinnati Row by a dense growth of bramble that effectively prevented foot traffic between the two socially separate ends of the island. Pete always had plenty to do to keep himself busy, but, since no Elliot Row people were even close to his age, he was naturally curious about the ones on the other side of the bramble barricade. From all he could see, though, they sure were different. He'd never seen any of them do anything but sail, read, or lie along the beach in the sun. Pete had never sailed, but he couldn't imagine it ever holding a candle to catching fish.

Pete propped his feet up on the edge of the *Tiny Tin* and watched as several sailboats were being readied for action in front of the Cincinnati Row boathouses. Each was exactly the same size, twenty-five feet long with a single mast and two sails. People, mostly his age, he guessed, were scrambling around on the decks shoving long, thin sticks into the white canvas sheets. Pete knew from previous years they would practice all week and then meet Saturday at noon for a race. In the next edition of the *Les Cheneaux Weekly Wave*, across the page from the fishing report, there would be a picture of the winning boat and its smiling crew. He'd often envisioned himself in those pictures.

Pete glanced behind him at the mainland shore. The *Tiny Tin* had reached the small, wooden building with the weathered letters that read, *FINNISH STEAM BATH*, the point beyond which they never caught any fish. Pete's dad turned to double back along the shore for a second pass at the Islington dock.

"I'd sure like to know where that bath begins," Howard was in the middle of saying for about the thousandth time when, WHAM, WHAM, WHAM, Pete's rod bent double and was almost jerked out of his hands. The line screamed off his reel as the crank handle spun backwards in a blur.

"I got one!" Pete yelled. He held his thumb on the spool to slow the fish, but it was like he'd hooked a torpedo. It peeled the line off his reel so fast that it immediately blistered his thumb.

His dad shoved the throttle lever to *Stop* and reeled in his lure to land the fish, but this one had no intention of coming in at all, much less any time soon. Pete's heart was pounding in his throat.

Mr. Jenkins glanced around to check the water and weather conditions. Fortunately, the wind would blow them into the channel away from the weeds and rocks of the nearby mainland shore. The line was still whizzing out when suddenly, forty yards behind the boat, an enormous fish flew out of the water, shaking its gaping jaws trying to throw the hook. Pete had never seen a pike jump like that.

"Keep your rod tip up! I think it's a muskie!"

A muskie! Holy Cow! Pete had never even seen a muskie.

As they slowly drifted away from the shelter of the mainland shore, the *Tiny Tin* began to bob like a cork in the gusting breeze. The strong wind would soon blow them into the Cincinnati Row shore crashing them into the rocks and boathouses.

Every time Pete took one turn on the crank, the fish jerked and spun more line from the reel. Pete's left hand began to cramp from the constant strain. As he held on, he realized that the fish was pulling the boat back toward the Finnish Steam Bath *against the wind.* The fish then turned another ninety degrees dragging the *Tiny Tin* along the channel toward Cedarville.

Pete switched the reel to his right hand. As he did, the line went slack. The pole snapped straight out and Pete's line dropped softly into the lake. He'd lost him.

Pete's heart dropped into his shoes.

"Start reeling!" his dad said.

Pete began to crank in the line. He couldn't believe he'd lost him. Just like that. One second on, the next second off. No flying out of the water. No tangling in underwater cover. Nothing. Just gone. Soon the spool was practically as full as when he had made his cast. Any second the old, scratched lure would pop out of the water and they'd start all over.

Tug.

Something pulled on Pete's line.

The pole, once again, bent double and pointed straight down underneath the boat. "I've still got him," Pete yelled.

Howard Jenkins reached for an oar and dipped it into the water next to Pete's line spinning the stern out of the way.

The reel handle spun backwards once again. This time the fish went straight for the sailboat in front of a Cincinnati Row boathouse. For the first time, Pete noticed the two boys and the girl who were rigging the sails on the mahogany sailboat. They stopped what they were doing to watch the show.

And some show it must have been. Here's a man and a boy dressed up in turn-of-the-century clothes getting tossed around in a little tin boat by waves that could easily capsize them or slam them into the rocks. They're being dragged around by some unseen force that's pulling them up and down and all over the channel. Fishing might not be an activity that these kids would ever care to include in their social calendars, but, when such an extraordinary exhibition is presented in their own front yard, they wouldn't miss watching it for the world. Now, whatever it was that had started the show was evidently coming their way.

Pete knew enough about sailboats to know that they had keels, and he would have to keep his fish away from this sailboat's keel or it would snap his line in an instant.

"You've got to draw him out of there, Pete," his dad said. "I'll row to keep us off shore." He jammed the oars into the oarlocks and strained against the waves.

"Bring him in," the sandy-haired boy on the sailboat smiled. "We want to see him."

Pete looked up. "I'm trying," he laughed. But then he wondered whether the kid was trying to be funny or if he was just plain ignorant. In the ten years Pete had been coming to the cottage, this was the first exchange he had ever had with anyone from Cincinnati Row. For all he knew, they might all be stupid.

He cranked hard and the spool continued to fatten. "I think he's almost in, Dad. You'd better get ready."

Mr. Jenkins stopped rowing and reached for the net.

"He may have another run left, Pete. Be careful."

Six feet straight down Pete could see a long, thick darkness with a tiny flash of silver at its mouth. Pete's left hand was knotted in agony. The blister on his thumb had popped and was bleeding. Pete's dad slid the net in the water. Slowly, Pete raised the pole. He couldn't believe his eyes. It looked like a submarine. Mr. Jenkins made a swipe with the net and filled it up. The hook dropped from the muskie's snaggle-toothed mouth as the monstrous fish thrashed in the net. Pete's dad swung him into the boat.

Pete stood up and screamed, thrusting his fists to the sky. He was joined in his cheer by the three in the sailboat. The blond-haired girl had a camera and was yelling, "Hold him up."

"Grab a cushion, Pete," his dad said. "Help me hold him down."

Mr. Jenkins reached behind the seat and flipped open the tackle box. Grabbing a hunting knife, he plunged the blade through the muskie's wide back, just behind its head. Blood shot out and the fish became still, its mouth open and its head protruding through a gaping hole in the net.

Pete had to stand to raise the forty-pound, sixty-inch fish from the floor of the *Tiny Tin* to show his audience on the sailboat. It took both hands just to lift it. He looked up and saw another forty people standing along the Cincinnati Row shore. As Pete grinned, they began to clap and cheer.

The blond-haired girl on the sailboat held a camera and yelled, "Smile," as if Pete had to be prompted, and she snapped the shutter. Pete glanced down at his dad who was as excited as Pete.

This would be a moment they would remember forever.

Pa Double Bottoms

CHAPTER 4
CELEBRATION

10:00 a.m.

As Pete carried the fish up the hill, word crackled like a lit fuse along Elliot Row. By the time he reached his cottage, everyone, including most of the hotel guests, were there to greet him. The head fishing guide brought a scale and calibrated pole to measure the enormous muskie. The hotel photographer snapped the official photo with Pete on one side of the fish staring into the camera like the old post card fishermen, while his dad smiled standing on the other side. Everyone else posed behind them grinning like they had just taken part in a momentous occasion—a rare event like the coronation of a king.

After Pete had told the entire fishing story, a distinguished gentleman approached Howard Jenkins and introduced himself.

"Hello, I'm James Barnwell," he said. "I just arrived from Mackinac Island. I met a client there who spoke so highly of this area that I decided to see it for myself before I returned to Los Angeles. Well, I'm sure glad I did. Nothing like this in California. And I've never seen so much excitement over one fish. I'll tell you what. Suppose I offer your son forty dollars, a dollar a pound, to buy it. Tonight, your family can join me and all the hotel guests in the formal dining room for a muskie dinner."

"Well," Mr. Jenkins said, "you'll have to ask the fisherman himself, but it sounds like a pretty generous offer to me." He looked over at Pete, "What do you say, Pete?"

"Forty dollars?" Pete exclaimed. "You bet. Besides, we couldn't eat this baby in a month, even if it did fit in our ice box." Pete lifted the muskie by the stringer and held it out to Mr. Barnwell.

The Californian smiled broadly as he reached into his coat pocket. He extracted a wallet, opened it, and handed Pete two, crisp, twenty dollar bills. "Here you are, Pete," Mr. Barnwell said beaming. "I took the liberty to ask the hotel chef to accompany me. This is Monsieur BerHale," Mr. Barnwell said motioning to a large man wearing a clean, white jacket and tall, chef's hat. "He'll return your stringer after he's dressed the fish."

In a flash, Pete remembered the events of the previous day and looked carefully at the two bills. "Dad," Pete whispered to his father. "These are fake. See the serial numbers? They're identical. It's just like at the gas station in Grayling. I think I saw one at the Bon Air, too."

Pete's dad looked at the two twenties. "Mr. Barnwell," he began, "there's something I believe you should know. I hope I'm wrong, but this money appears to be counterfeit. Pete seems to think there's a lot of it around lately."

Mr. Barnwell spread the two twenties in his hands. His jaw dropped. "I must have gotten them on Mackinac Island as change from my hotel bill." He reached back into his wallet and withdrew four $10 bills which he looked at very carefully. "Here," he said to Howard, "I'll report this right away. I don't know what I'd have done if I had tried to buy something in town and been caught spending one of these. I own a publishing company, you see. I print books, not currency. I am now, more than ever, indebted to you," he said, regaining some of his composure. "Will I see you and your family tonight for dinner?"

"You sure will," Pete said, folding the money.

With that, a red-faced Mr. Barnwell along with the hotel chef and the biggest muskie ever caught in the Les Cheneaux Islands turned and departed down the path toward the hotel.

———

Pete went to the back porch wash stand to clean up. He was blood and fish scales from head to toe. As he dried his face, he remembered the sailboat race the Cincinnati Row kids were practicing for that morning. He decided he'd put on some clean clothes and watch it from the end of the Elliot Hotel dock. After pulling a fresh tee-shirt over his head, he grabbed his lucky captain's cap and started along the path toward the Elliot.

"Way to go, Pete," Arlouine Henny said as he passed her going to the well.

"Great fish, Pete," Russell Patrick called out from his porch.

Pete nodded and smiled to the tall, leathery-faced man.

"Good going," Mrs. Wirtle said as he walked by her yellow cottage.

20

Even Mr. Eberline, the manager of the Islington Hotel, and Mr. Blome, the owner of the Elliot, stopped their conversation and nodded to Pete as he made his way past them and started down the wide, wooden steps to the Elliot pier.

Halfway down the stairs, Pete caught sight of the mahogany sailboat that he'd seen the blond-haired girl and the two boys rigging that morning. Pete strode quickly out to the end of the dock and leaned up against a telephone pole-sized piling where he watched them practicing their turns.

Shortly before noon, a man aboard the race committee boat, the *Polly Ann*, dropped white markers in a wide ring around Elliot Bay and set two red flags, side-by-side, off the end of the Elliot dock. Ten sailboats gathered nearby for the final instructions. The boats were to circle the course three times. The finish line would be the two markers right in front of Pete. Pete recognized the *Polly Ann* as a boat that was kept in one side of the red double boathouse where he had landed his muskie.

Just before the starting gun, the three sailors guided their entry, the *Griffin*, over toward Pete. He watched as each tossed a penny into the water, apparently for good luck.

The girl glanced up and saw Pete. She looked terrific in her white bathing suit and her long hair blowing in the warm breeze. She smiled and motioned to the two boys who turned their heads and waved. The dark-complexioned, curly-haired boy called out, "Stick around. It's our turn to put on a show for you. We're going to win this race."

Pete waved back, too surprised to say anything. Maybe they weren't stupid, after all.

"Wish some of your good luck on us," the

smaller, blond-haired boy said. "Eddie's got more confidence than my sister and I put together."

"Danny and Kate wouldn't know a winning sailboat if they were sitting on it, which they are," Eddie laughed. "But wish us luck, anyhow."

The race began with a pistol shot from the *Polly Ann*. The *Griffin* struggled through the first two laps but as they passed the Elliot dock to start the third leg, Pete, remembering what the blond-haired boy had called out to him as he was fighting the muskie, grinned and yelled out, "Go faster."

Dan smiled back and gave Pete the thumbs up as though this was a piece of strategy they had somehow overlooked. They tried it and it worked. The *Griffin* crossed the finish line a second ahead of a white-hulled sloop that had led the entire race. The winning team guided their boat back to Pete and the dark-haired captain grinned and called out, "Thanks, that was brilliant. Next week, we'll have to try it right from the gun. See you later." And off the three sailed back toward Cincinnati Row.

———

Later that afternoon, Pete and Cara went into town to do their regular errands. "I'll get the mail, Pete," Cara said as they went ashore. "You can go to the Bon Air and get us a table. Dad gave me an extra dollar to celebrate your muskie. We'll do the groceries later."

Pete could already picture the menu board behind the mirrored fountain. It listed a dozen selections, including sundaes, sodas, phosphates, malts, floats, and banana splits, all of which ranged from five to thirty-five cents. But everybody's favorite was the house special: the forty-five cent Jersey Mud. Over the years, Pete had heard them being ordered and watched them being made, but he had never had one. The prospect of diving into a Jersey Mud was almost more than he could stand. Pete and Cara's daily trip to town for mail and supplies was normally rewarded with their choice of nickel candy sold at the Bon Air counter. Cara usually bought a Charleston Chew which she took home and set on the ice block. After dinner she'd smash it on the floor and share the pieces with everyone, even Pete, provided he knelt at her feet and begged like a dog. She was such a pain.

Pete, on the other hand, always got a Holloway Sucker which he could make last all day. He'd wrap and unwrap it a dozen times between baiting hooks and cleaning fish before it finally disappeared leaving only a grimy, wooden stick and disgustingly filthy wrapper.

But today was special, perhaps the most special day in Pete's life. He had caught a trophy fish, sold it for a huge sum of forty dollars, and become a hero in the process. He had met three people his own age, one of whom was the prettiest girl he had ever seen, and now he was about to waltz into the Bon Air to order up the fruit of unholy sin, a Jersey Mud.

With any luck at all, and this seemed to be Pete's day for that, his new friends would already be there celebrating their sailing victory. They would offer him a seat and the rest of the summer would be the best ever.

Pete had the entire scenario, dialogue included, summed up by the time he reached the Bon Air's screen door.

Cedarville

CHAPTER 5
THE SECOND CATCH

2:00 p.m.

Pete opened the screen door and stopped dead in his tracks. No one was there.

Mrs. Clark, standing behind the soda fountain, read his mind. "How come you're not up at the high school for the big softball game, Pete? It starts in fifteen minutes."

Softball game? Pete immediately thought of his dad's high school teachers' picnics where the teams consisted of about thirty men, women, and children spread out over a pasture and would last until the hot dogs were cooked. This would be a great chance to meet some people.

"Thanks," Pete said, and he pushed open the Bon Air door. Cara was just coming out of the post office as Pete rushed up. "Cara, there's a softball game about to start at the high school. What say we go over?"

"Go on ahead. I'll do the errands and meet you up there."

"Thanks, Cara," Pete called after her, "I don't care what they say behind your back. You're not all bad." He got her that time. Boy, this was his day.

Pete ran to the end of Hodeck Street where the road turns up to the high school. In the distance he could see over a hundred people gathered near the backstop. As he passed through the outfield toward home plate, he slowed to a walk, trying to assess the situation.

Along the third base line nine men stood dressed in old baseball uniforms and wearing spikes. They were whipping softballs back and forth, the slap of leather being the only sound coming from that side of the field. All were high school age or older with a few women sitting on the three-tiered set of wooden bleachers behind them.

Across the way, down the first base line were boys and girls, men and women, babies and grandparents, all dressed to the teeth sporting either Cincinnati Reds or Chicago White Sox baseball caps. A few had baseball gloves, but most did not. Shiny white softballs were being lobbed softly back and forth. The chatter was animated and incessant:

"Nice throw, Stella."

"Over here, Gretta."

"Good catch, Charley."

"Toss a pop-up to me, Alice."

"Give me a grounder, Kip, but not so hard this time."

It was evident that a massacre was about to begin.

Pete spotted the three *Griffin* sailboat kids, the two boys standing sixty feet apart throwing hard to each other. The girl, looking Pete's way, stood next to the sandy-haired boy. She waved to Pete and nudged her brother. He looked up and motioned for Pete to come over.

"Hey," he said, "would you like to play? If you catch softballs like you catch fish, we might have a chance."

Pete walked over deciding that this wouldn't be the time to mention the obvious; these guys had only one chance, unconditional surrender.

"Sure," he replied, "but I didn't bring my glove. I'm Pete. Pete Jenkins."

"Don't worry, Pete, we'll find one for you. I'm Danny Hinken. This is my twin sister, Kate." Dan was Pete's size, 5'9" and wiry. Kate was an inch or two shorter but pretty beyond words. Pete tried his best to look casually disinterested as he smiled and nodded her way.

"Down there is Eddie," Dan continued, "Eddie Terkel. Okay, Pete, let's see what you can do. For now, try using my glove." Dan handed his glove to Pete and tossed the ball to Eddie who was decidedly bigger, taller, and stronger than anyone else on the field. He wore a huge smile like a flag of truce.

Eddie called to Pete, "You ready?"

"I guess," Pete said working his fingers into the mitt. Eddie tossed one in, chest high. Pete caught it and snapped it back.

For the next several throws, Eddie gave Pete a real workout firing balls everywhere but right to him. Pete caught them all but remained unsure as to whether Eddie was testing him or just a terrible thrower.

"I've seen enough," Dan said. "What do you play?"

"Well," Pete said, not wanting to upset whatever person's feelings he evidently was about to replace, "usually I play first base, but I just got here. There's lots of people ahead of me. Maybe I should wait for awhile."

"Hey," Dan said. "We've got eight good players here, and now, you make nine."

"That's right," Eddie added, as he joined his friends. "All these other people usually play in this game. But not today. The Cedarville team has thumped us every year for as long as even my grandfather can remember. They're all local men and they figure this is their turf. When the game starts this time though, all of our little kids and parents will slip quietly into the bleachers and we'll have ourselves an honest-to-goodness ball game.

"Every year," Eddie said, "some of us can be here. Some of us can't. It doesn't take but one weak spot in the field, and we're lunch. Those guys can tattoo their names on a wall from a hundred feet."

"If we put one second-rate fielder out there," Dan added, "they'll find him and run him ragged. Meanwhile, the rest of us stand around watching the shellac dry. Last summer, after being drubbed by about twenty runs, we got together and talked our parents into arranging their vacations so we could all be here at the same time. Everyone's here except our first baseman, Neal Preston. He won't be up for a couple of weeks. We had no one to fill his spot until now. It looks, Pete, like you're the missing link."

Pete glanced around quickly re-assessing his teammates. The eight real ballplayers were completely camouflaged. Dan was right. This would be no ordinary picnic softball game.

The umpire, Cedarville High football coach, Bill Ebinger, pulled down his face mask, dusted off home plate, and hollered, "Play ball!"

The game was on. The Cedarville nine took the field and immediately set the resorters down 1-2-3.

When Pete and his friends took their defensive positions and there were no little kids on the field, the Cedarville guys quickly realized that the resorters meant business. They also were set down in order.

In the top of the second, Eddie Terkel led off and, after flexing his muscles, leaned into a waist-high spinner and sent it into Cedarville Bay. He trotted around the bases with his bear-in-a-bee-hive grin to put the cottagers ahead, one to nothing.

For the next five innings, neither team could push a runner past third base. It came down to the bottom of the last and the Cedarville men still trailed the islanders by one.

Duke Armour, the resorters' pitcher, got the first batter on a ground ball to Moose Harding at short who flipped it to Pete for an easy out. One away. Then the Cedarville pitcher, Con Shoberg, blooped a single to left. The center fielder, Bob Arfstrom, followed with a slicing double down the left field line to put runners on second and third with only one out. A single here would easily drive in two runs and put the resorters back into their three-generations-long misery of losing the annual game to the locals.

The Cedarville catcher, left-handed hitting John Torsky, strode smugly to the plate. He had ripped shots past Pete down the first base line on each of his three at-bats, two for doubles and one for a triple. Duke Armour grooved the first pitch and Torsky blasted a rope that headed for right field between Pete and Steve Brumleve at second. Pete dived to his right and snared the ball an inch off the ground. He rolled over keeping his glove high in the air. The umpire raised his arm, "Batter's out!" he bellowed.

Pete scrambled to his feet and fired a strike to Chip Williams at third who stepped on the bag before the lead runner could slide back in.

The ump raised his arm a second time and the bleachers along first base erupted in wild jubilation.

Pete was immediately mobbed by a hundred people yipping and whooping as if they'd just won the World Series. When the dust finally settled and Pete had shaken everyone's hand for about the third time, someone yelled out, "Jersey Muds on me." The crowd raced across center field toward town.

Pete realized he was long overdue to meet Cara. He looked around and there she was, standing alone by the backstop.

CHAPTER 6
THE MYSTERY

5:30 p.m.

As Pete and Cara walked back to town, Pete looked up and saw his three friends standing in front of the post office. "Cara, let's hurry," Pete said, "I think they're waiting for us."

"Are you two coming to the Bon Air?" Eddie asked.

"We've got to get back, Pete," Cara replied quickly. "We've been invited to have dinner at the Elliot Hotel," she explained to the other three. "We're due in an hour."

"We'll make it another time then," Dan said. "Say, we've been wondering. For years you two have gone past our place every day going into town. Your cottage must be down beyond the Elliot dock."

"That's right," Pete said. "How'd you know?"

"Well," Dan said, "you always drive your boat along our side of the channel. If you lived anywhere else, you'd probably follow the other shoreline. It only matters because we'd like to know

30

about the old man who lives on the little island down that way."

"Mr. Geetings?" Pete replied. "Oh, he's just an old hermit. My mom knew him years ago, but she told me never to bother him. Lives there year 'round, I guess."

"Why do you want to know?" Cara asked.

"Well," Eddie began, "an awful lot of strange things have been going on around here lately. And the more we think about it, the more they all involve that old coot."

"To begin with," Dan continued, "early last summer he started getting lots of small boxes in the mail. He must have carted a dozen of them out to his boat in one week. After that, about every week or so, he'd receive two large cartons and haul them back to his little island. That went on all summer. Last week Eddie, Kate, and I made a night sail on the *Griffin* to Mackinac. We came into the harbor about midnight and passed this unbelievable speedboat. It was long and wide and low with a black hull and mahogany deck. The moon shone on it as clear as day. We could see someone else sitting in the shadows, but it was that old man at the helm."

"And this speedboat," Eddie added, "as big and powerful as it looked, didn't make a sound as it passed us in the harbor. It just gurgled, like water being drawn into a bathtub. We started to pull the *Griffin* into the slip he had just left, but a tall, skinny guy was standing right there and told us the space was reserved. We came about and the old man was still heading silently toward the shipping channel. As soon as he got beyond the breakwall, he hit the throttle and shot off like a rocket."

"In two seconds," Dan added, "he disappeared heading straight for the Snows."

"We've seen him a thousand times in town," Eddie continued, "but we never thought anything about him. Just a plain old man. But that speed-boat. It just doesn't add up."

"And then yesterday," Kate added, "we were at the Bon Air. It was about two o'clock. He came in and got change from Jack Frazier, the soda jerk. He made a quick call from the pay phone and left through the front door."

"About ten minutes later," Dan continued, "Mrs. Clark, the owner, came in and rang up a sale for a customer. She got angry, went to her office and made a phone call. Then she went over to Jack and showed him the bill, but he just shrugged his shoulders. She was hopping mad. She tacked it to a wall next to a couple others just like it. Look around town. Almost every store has one or two twenty dollar bills hung up by their office."

"In short," Dan said glancing at Cara," we think he's making counterfeit money over there on that little island, but we can't get anyone to listen to us."

Cara shook her head. "I think you all must be mistaken. How could somebody have a boat like that around here for two summers and no one ever see it? Besides, you just said that when you landed at Mackinac Island, it was dark. It could have been anyone in that boat."

The five walked into town. Pete and Cara split off at Hossack's to go to their boat while the others headed for the celebration at the Bon Air. Pete's Jersey Mud would just have to wait for another day. ———

The dinner at the Elliot was a major event. All the hotel guests were dressed up and James

32

Barnwell, the California publisher, toasted Pete for making the fish dinner possible. When the salad was finished, Chef BerHale threw open the kitchen door displaying Pete's muskie on a magnificent silver tray. Pete about lost it when he saw the muskie's head was still attached, the lip torn where he'd been hooked. Pete wondered what else this big time chef might have forgotten. ——

Ordinarily, after Pete had caught a big fish, he would be able to think of little else for a week, especially at bedtime. This night, however, as he crawled between the thick sheets, he barely gave the muskie a thought. All of the day's other events spun through his head: the softball game, the sailboat race, his new friends, the fake money, Mr. Geetings and his speedboat.

Just as he was dozing off, he became aware of a low-pitched drone. He stood up next to his bed and looked out over the moon-flooded Elliot Bay just as a long, sleek boat cruised in towards the old man's island. It quickly disappeared in the dense growth of reeds surrounding the hidden shore.

As Pete stood looking through the wavy glass window, a bolt of lightning and a deafening crash of thunder exploded outside. Rain came down in sheets. The sky darkened and his view of Mr. Geetings' island became obscured in the pitch black of the storm. Pete turned to his bed, his mind racing, and crawled back in.

Mystery Island

CHAPTER 7
WEATHERED IN

Sunday, June 15   6:30 a.m.

Pete awakened the next morning to the steady drum of heavy rain beating on the cottage roof. Ordinarily, he would cozy back in his warm bed and alternately sleep or read until the weather cleared. This morning though, Pete felt more than a twinge of frustration. He was anxious to tell his friends about the speedboat, but with the rain coming in buckets, he wouldn't even be able to get past his front porch, much less down to his boat and all the way to Cincinnati Row.

He bumped the double bed next to his. "Hey, Cara, are you awake?" he whispered.

"No."

"Listen, I'm serious. Remember what those Cincinnati Row kids said yesterday about Mr. Geetings? I saw a boat come into his island last night. It was just like they said. It was a long, low speedboat. I watched it from Reif's Point all the way to the back of his island." He paused for a response. "Did you hear me?"

34

"No. Go away. Let me sleep. You're spoiling a perfectly good, rainy day."

Pete bounced out of his bunk and into a pair of jeans. Maybe he could learn something from his mother. He slipped through the curtain doorway into the living room and found his mom in the kitchen putting strips of bacon into a cast iron frying pan over the gas stove.

"Mom. What do you know about Mr. Geetings?"

"Harold Geetings?" she asked. "Oh, he was quite the dandy in his day. When I was a young girl, he was a top student at the University of Chicago. He and his parents would stay the whole summer at the Elliot Hotel. Harold was always writing poems and stories about all the people along Elliot Row. That little scrap of birch bark with the words penned on it is Harold's doing. You know, the one in the living room with the pipe tied to it."

Pete remembered. It was tacked next to the map of the islands. It read:

> *This old corn pipe of cob and clay*
> *Is good for many ills, they say,*
> *But, of this, I'm very sure,*
> *For asthma, it's a certain cure.*

"Well," Averill Jenkins continued, "his mother had asthma, and the Les Cheneaux Islands was the only place she could get relief during the summer. A lot of people came up here because of that. That's why I started coming, you know, to help Grandma Drake. Our families were very close so she and Grandma Heidelberg invited me to stay every summer from the time I was twelve until I went away to college. What wonderful summers those were.

35

"So," she went on, "Harold Geetings' mother got along fine up here during the summer. But one May, back in Chicago, she had a terrible asthma attack and died. Harold's father was heartbroken. He mourned terribly, lost his health, and passed away himself the very next year. His will left Harold a sizeable fortune. Harold bought that little island and built the cabin the same year. He's lived there summer and winter ever since.

"At first, he'd have wonderful parties inviting all of his Elliot Row friends. He would ask us to tell him all about ourselves. He'd laugh, scribble pages of notes, and insisted that, one day, he'd write a book about each one of us. Nothing ever came of it though. As the years went by, he withdrew from us completely. Once we surprised him by rowing over with all the fixings for a party. When we arrived, he was sitting at his desk, papers everywhere. He said he was writing a novel and he didn't have time for such foolishness. He sent us away making it clear he didn't want to be bothered with our visits ever again. So, from then on, we've just left him alone.

"Odd that you should mention him though," she said turning the bacon in the frying pan. "Friday, when we arrived in Cedarville, I saw him coming out of the post office carrying two large boxes. I said, `Hello,' but he ignored me. He was all dressed up, too, something I hadn't seen him do for ages. I asked Mr. Visnaw, the postmaster, about him. He said that word around town was that he finally sold a novel. Someone even saw him at a marina in Charlevoix last year looking at speedboats. When I saw him leave the Cedarville dock, though, he was still using the same wooden outboard that he's had for thirty years."

Pete's mom paused a moment, holding a carton of eggs and gazing out the cabin window. "There was something different about him. I can't put my finger on it, but he seemed frightened."

After removing the bacon and lowering the flame, she cracked open eight eggs and set them sizzling in the pan. Pete told her, as nonchalantly as he could, what his friends had seen at the Mackinac Island marina.

"Sounds to me, if it actually was Harold Geetings they saw, that he was successful with a novel," Mrs. Jenkins said. "Nothing terribly mysterious about that. It's wonderful news. My advice to you, Peter, is to leave him alone and tend to your own business."

"We're just curious, Mom," Pete said.

Howard Jenkins came in the back door with an armful of logs for the wood stove. He shook the rain from his hat and hung it on the hook.

"It looks like your mother's got breakfast about ready, Pete," he said carrying the logs into the living room. "How about going in and prying your sister out of bed?"

Pete got up from the kitchen chair, walked to his room, and bounced his sister's bed. "Cara, breakfast is ready."

"Pete, I heard what Mom told you," she whispered in a slow, measured tone. "Listen to me very carefully. I don't want to spend my whole summer looking out after you. You'd better leave that old man alone like Mom says or I'll give you an arm-twisting like you've never had before. Do you understand?"

Pete winced. He could feel his wrist cracking already.

The downpour continued all day with Pete taking turns reading in his bunk or watching the rain from the front porch swing. In the afternoon he worked a jigsaw puzzle with his mom and helped his dad oil the fishing reels. He made up a ping-pong basketball game that he played for an hour nearly driving Cara to distraction. After dinner she got back at him whipping him five out of six at double-solitaire. Later, they made popcorn and roasted marshmallows in the wood stove.

Still the rain pelted the Straits area. Pete's misery became complete when his dad won two games out of three at cribbage and declared that he could no longer, in good conscience, take advantage of a child at a man's game. He feigned boredom for the ease of his victory. Pete did a slow burn knowing that his dad had pegged out in the rubber game leaving him in the stink hole with sixteen points in his hand and the first count. But Pete knew the cardinal rule of cribbage: "Winning is only half the game. It's how you gloat, that counts."

Tomorrow would be another day.

Pea Coulee Boathouse

CHAPTER 8
FISHING LESSON

Monday, June 16 6:30 a.m.

Pete woke up early the next morning. The drumming on the roof had stopped. It was barely light so it was way too early to call on his friends in Cincinnati Row. Pete's thoughts naturally went to fishing. As long as he was up, he might as well get an early start on the lake.

He slipped into his parents bedroom and whispered to his dad. "Want to go fishing?"

"Not this morning, Pete. I had a meeting with all the big ones down at the dock last night and they've asked me to give them a break. But you go ahead, I don't think they'll mind."

"All right, Dad, I guess I'll just have to get my muskie's big brother all by myself."

Pete dressed and hurried down the hill to the dock. He bailed out the *Tiny Tin* and headed across Elliot Bay over to Islington Point. He decided he'd fish along the mainland shore across from Cincinnati Row and watch for any action near the red double boathouse. If one of his friends came out, he'd casually troll over and say hello. Then he'd pass along the news about Mr. Geetings and the mystery boat.

About 9:30, Pete saw someone standing on the shore where he believed Dan and Kate lived. He cut across the channel and began to fish along the Cincinnati Row boathouses. Pete heard a screen door slam from behind the trees and Kate came running out to the end of the dock. She was wearing a bright yellow sun dress, matching sandals, and a smile that could melt rocks.

"Catch anything, Pete?" she called out. Pete's heart jumped into his throat. He could hardly reach around fast enough to lift his stringer of three northern pike. Just then another screen door slammed. Dan and Eddie trotted down the short dock to join Kate.

"Wow!" Dan said, seeing Pete's display. "How about taking us fishing?"

"Really?" Pete said surprised that any of them would be interested. "Sure, but you'd better get changed. It's likely to get pretty messy."

"All right," Dan said for the three of them. "Tie up behind my outboard. We'll be back in five minutes."

Pete started the little Chris-Craft motor and pulled in just ahead of Dan's brand new, red and white Lyman boat that had been outfitted with a Fastwin Evinrude engine. It was at least twice the size of the *Tiny Tin*.

Pete heard a screen door spring shut and again, out from the woods, came his friends. None of them looked as if they were about to go fishing, however. They were dressed more for an afternoon of croquet or tennis.

40

As the three looked down into the *Tiny Tin*, Eddie said with a grin, "Do you think we'll all fit? I'm afraid I'll swamp her."

"Eddie's right. Let's take Dan's boat," Kate suggested.

"Fine with me," Dan agreed. "What do you say, Pete?"

Pete glanced over at Dan's outboard. He'd never fished from any other boat than the *Tiny Tin*. He had never trolled with a motor other than the five-horse Chris-Craft. Dan's boat was longer than his, and wider. The seats were different. It was all wrong. It was a disaster waiting to happen. On the other hand, it was the only way he was going to show Kate what a terrific fisherman he was.

"Great," Pete said.

The four quickly piled into Dan's new boat. "I'll drive the first leg, Pete," Dan offered. "You can get Eddie and Kate set up for fishing."

Dan started her up and brought the motor down to trolling speed. He lined the red and white Lyman up to pass close to the shore in front of the Cincinnati Row boathouses.

"All right," Pete said smiling like a teacher on the first day of school. "Who wants to be first?"

Kate picked up one of the two poles and assessed the reel mechanism. "You'd better start with Eddie," she said. "I'll watch while you show him how it's done."

Eddie took the other rod and reel in his big hands. "I've done some deep sea fishing," he said shaking his head, "but I've never used one of these little rigs before."

Pete was under the impression that this was the only kind of rod and reel there was. Also, he had forgotten how long it had taken him to learn the techniques of casting, letting out line, adjusting the drag, and all the other stuff it takes just to get the lure wet. Pete flipped the Dardevle out to the port side, handed the rod to Eddie, and showed him how to keep his thumb on the spool. Then he turned his attention to Kate who was watching intently from the bow.

"Now I'll get you set up, Kate. First, you'd better sit here beside Eddie or your line will get caught in the prop."

"This looks pretty easy," she replied moving to the middle seat.

"Yep, there's nothing to it," Pete said casually as he cast Kate's silver spoon out to the starboard.

"This is so exciting," she beamed, taking the pole from Pete. "I might just catch a muskie bigger than the one you got the other day."

"Anything can happen," Pete agreed. "That's the great part about fishing. You just never—"

Kate's rod bent double and the reel spun backwards. "What's happening?" she screamed. In a second, a backlash fouled the spool. She grasped one hand to the middle of the pole and clenched the other to the handle.

Pete grabbed the rod before the whole shebang was yanked into the lake. "Cut the motor, Dan!" Pete yelled. "Reel in your line, Eddie! Kate, keep your thumb on the spool."

"Here! You take it!" Kate shrieked, jamming the pole into Pete's chest.

As Pete grabbed the handle, the fish took off in the other direction. Predictably, the line snapped. The whole incident took less than five seconds.

The four friends sat staring at each other. No one knew whether to laugh or cry. Pete, the bigtime fishing guide, was in over his head, fortunately only figuratively.

"I think you had a big one, Kate," Pete smiled finally. "It's all my fault. I tried to show you too much too fast."

"Oh, Pete," Kate said. "You weren't kidding. That was exciting."

"Would you like to try again?" Pete asked.

"No. I'll let Dan have a turn. I'll just watch from the bow for awhile." She made her way to the front of the boat and removed her swimwear cover-up revealing a bright red, two piece bathing suit. As Eddie and Dan situated themselves on the middle seat, Pete moved to the back to steer the boat. He became totally unraveled as Kate arranged three cushions across the bow and arched her back against the port gunwale.

She stretched her legs over the starboard and closed her eyes to the warm sun.

"If you can fix that bird's nest in the spool, Pete, I'd like to go next," Dan said interrupting Pete's trance.

"Oh, yeah, sure. Hand me my tackle box," Pete replied, his mind only marginally on fishing.

An hour passed and the only luck they had was that all four were still aboard and Pete's view was better than any other guy's in all of Mackinac County.

"What do you say we call it a morning," Dan said checking his watch. "My mother's expecting us for lunch at noon. You're invited, Pete."

"Thanks, but I'd better get home," Pete said.

"The next lesson is yours, Pete," Eddie announced after Dan made his landing in front of the *Tiny Tin*. "Come on back at two o'clock and we'll teach you how to sail."

43

"All right," Pete brightened. "I'll see you then. Sorry about our fishing luck. We'll try again, okay?"

"Okay, Pete," Dan said. "See you at two."

Pete was stowing his fishing gear when he remembered the mystery boat.

"I forgot to tell you the news," Pete said. "I saw that speedboat you told me about. It came in to Mr. Geeting's island two nights ago. It was just like you said. Maybe we should swing over and see if it's still there."

Kate's eyes brightened. "Are you kidding? You saw it come in? Let's go right now!"

"We'd better have lunch first," Eddie suggested. "We'll sail around that way this afternoon in the *Griffin*. If anyone is on that island, they wouldn't expect someone on a sailboat would be spying on them."

Pete untied the two lines holding the *Tiny Tin* to the dock. "I'll be back at two," he said pulling the starter cord.

The tin boat lurched forward and Pete was on his way home. He turned and waved to the threesome who then headed for shore, each with a fishing lesson behind him and anxious for the afternoon spying mission ahead.

CHAPTER 9
THE TRAIL

1:00 p.m.

Pete learned at lunch that his mom and sister needed the *Flossy* to go into town, and his dad was going to use the *Tiny Tin* to repair their dock. So, if Pete was going sailing, he'd have to walk to Cincinnati Row. He'd never hiked beyond the Elliot Hotel before, but he'd been to the end of the path many times where dense bramble grew wild.

For Pete to visit his friends that afternoon, he must somehow pass the impassible. He remembered his dad's advice, "Pete," he said, "life is full of barriers. Some keep you out, some hold you in. It's easy to stay where you are, but if you really want to, you can find a way to the other side." Pete thought about Kate sunning herself on the bow of Dan's boat. He really wanted to. She wasn't just pretty. She was spunky and smart and fun to be with. As anxious as he had been at first to meet Dan and Eddie, his every thought now was centered on Kate.

Up and down the Elliot Hotel lot line Pete searched for a weak point in the dense shrubbery. Finally, along the side of the hotel's tool shed about thirty feet up from shore, Pete noticed a small gap. He pulled some overhanging foliage to one side, ducked low, and realized that he was in some sort of natural tunnel. He worked his way around for thirty feet or so and, coming to the end, brushed aside a few more branches. He stood up and found himself in totally different surroundings.

He had done it. He was in Cincinnati Row. He turned around, picked up a sharp rock, and blazed two notches, eye level, on the closest trees to the passageway. He turned again and took in his new surroundings. It was like stepping onto another continent. There was no underbrush, only tall, green cedars. The forest floor was spongy with thick, gnarled roots poking through the mossy thatch. Heavy, moist air filled his lungs, and a cool, green, light permeated the atmosphere.

Pete began to pick his way over the soft terrain. Slowly, he became conscious of an ominous presence. He raised his eyes and found a dark, hotel-sized building a few feet to his right rising directly overhead. A small sign nailed to a tree read, *The Taj Ma-Snows*. He stood for a moment stunned. It was three stories tall with windows, balconies, cupolas, and decks facing Elliot Bay.

His first reaction was that of a trespasser: he'd better run or he'd be shot. As the wind blew through the cedars, he heard the cracking sound of a cartridge being slammed into a rifle chamber. He froze. In an instant, he'd be blasted from above. He thought again about Kate. They'd have to bring him down advancing. He wasn't about to turn back.

To his left, almost to shore, Pete noticed a path. There were ruts and roots and ridges, but Pete raced for it fully expecting that the next step would be his last. He dashed along, a mere five or ten feet from the lapping waves of the channel shoreline. Occasionally, he would feel a presence on his right of what must be another dwelling, although he dared not look. His gaze would certainly draw the attention of those in the turret towers inviting fire from its guarding marksmen.

At regular intervals, light poured through the trees and he would be blinded by the sun. He soon realized he was passing intersections to boathouses, structures he had seen a thousand times from the lake but never from land. He counted them off as he rushed by: the single white boathouse next to the Elliot; the first red, double boathouse; the single red; the triple green; the single brown. One more and he'd be there at the second, red, double boathouse.

As he approached it, Pete stopped in his tracks. At the foot of the dock, the path split and went up a gradual slope to two residences, each as impressive and imposing as the other. He guessed that one was Dan and Kate's and the other, Eddie's. He mentally flipped a coin and chose the one-story, baronial lodge to his left. It was somehow less forbidding than the taller one higher on the hill.

He stepped slowly up the stairs listening for a familiar voice. Finally, throwing caution aside, he rapped on the wooden screen door and stepped back, prepared to make a run for it.

"Who is it?" called a strong, deep voice from within.

Pete hesitated. Who should he ask for? What if he'd arrived at neither of their places?

"Is Dan or Eddie there?" he asked.

"Pete?" came a cheerful response from within. It was Dan. "We didn't hear your motor. Come in, we're just finishing lunch."

Pete drew a sigh of relief and pulled the knob on the screen door. He took one step inside and found he was on the threshold of the most remarkable room he'd ever seen. To his right was a spectacular stone fireplace that filled the entire cathedral-ceilinged wall. An oval, braided rug in front of it was surrounded by a semi-circle of wicker chairs.

Before he could even turn his head to see what lay at the other end of this immense room, Pete heard a chord played on a piano.

"Ta Da!" It was Kate. "Mom and Dad, this is Pete Jenkins. He catches baseballs and fish and this afternoon we're going to teach him how to catch the wind."

"Katherine, that's no way to introduce a guest," an extraordinarily attractive woman said as she approached.

"Hello, Peter," the lady continued pleasantly. "I'm Mrs. Hinken." Then she nodded to a man sitting in a chair by the fireplace. Closing a book, the man stood and turned to Pete as Mrs. Hinken continued, "and this is Doctor Hinken, Katherine and Daniel Junior's father."

Pete gasped audibly. He was thunderstruck. This one room was twice the size of the Jenkins' entire cottage. Pete avoided the eyes of the approaching man and looked further into the house. The dining room, although somewhat smaller, was even more elegant. The Hinkens had been dining at a long table set with crystal, silver, china, and real cloth napkins. There was no sign of rubber drinking cups or ceramic bowls collected from specially marked boxes of Quaker Oats cereal.

Pete's eyes darted up and around the walls. Trophy elk, deer, moose, and fish peeked out from the massive wooden beams crossing high overhead. Nothing was out of place. Not a fishing lure. Not a kernel of popcorn. Not a marshmallow stick. There were no *Baby Huey* or *Superman* or any other kind of comic books anywhere.

As Pete remained in the doorway, Dr. Hinken approached and extended his right hand. Pete could kick himself for ignoring his mother's suggestions to join the YMCA class that teaches basic etiquette to teenagers. "Oh, Mom, that's all old-fashioned stuff," he would tell her. "Nobody needs it anymore. That's for dukes and dukettes over in Eng-land, not for us kids in America." Ha. If he could get out of this old lodge even remotely socially alive, he'd start memorizing the manners book his mom was forever setting as a paperweight atop his stack of comics.

Dr. Hinken stood before Pete. Pete slowly lifted his clammy hand and felt it being grasped.

"Hi," Pete managed weakly, his eyes glazing over.

Dan grabbed Pete by the arm. "We'll be back in a couple of hours."

Pete felt like a Neanderthal, a sub-species he suddenly suspected had become extinct purely out of embarrassment. It was entirely possible that, in the presence of those clever new *Homo sapiens* who had just moved into the neighborhood, young Neanderthals just gave up and jumped into the nearest available tar pit. It made perfect sense to Pete.

"We'll be taking the *Griffin* to Urie Bay," Dan said to his parents as he headed for the door. "The

49

breeze is picking up, so it should be a pretty good sail. Let's go, Pete."

Pete managed a frail smile. "Take it easy," he mumbled to Dr. and Mrs. Hinken as the screen door slapped shut behind him.

"I think he's from Michigan," Kate said explaining her new friend's awkward behavior. "But he's nice enough, once you get to know him. Anyway, we won't be long."

She slipped out the door and caught up with Pete and her twin brother.

a little Dinghy

CHAPTER 10
THE SAILING LESSON

2:00 p.m.

Pete and Kate followed Dan to the side of the neighboring cottage. "Hey, Eddie!" Dan called in the direction of an open, second story window.

"Yes?" came a voice from within.

"We'll be at the *Griffin*," Dan called. "Don't forget the key."

Eddie pushed a curtain aside and poked his head out the window. "Please?" he said.

"Bring the key!" Dan repeated.

"Oh, okay. I'll be there in five minutes."

Please? Pete thought. *Please what? Was Eddie asking Dan for something? No. Dan was asking Eddie for the key. If anyone would be saying Please? it should be Dan.* Pete suspected that Cincinnatians said Please? instead of the more familiar terms Huh? or What? They sure were an odd lot. They didn't just have a funny accent, they had a whole nother way of talking.

Pete followed Kate down to the dock. Dan disappeared through a small door into the boathouse and reappeared from the other side in a small, green rowboat with *A Little Dinghy* inscribed on its stern.

"Hop aboard," Dan said to Pete and Kate. "I'll drop you off at the *Griffin* and then come back and wait for Eddie."

The dinghy had a thick white, rub rail all the way around it. Pete understood why after a few moments of trying to get himself out of it and onto the *Griffin*. It bobbed opposite to the sailboat, bumping into it with each wave.

"Watch," Kate instructed. "It's easy." She sprang deftly onto the sailboat as the dinghy surged from the trough of a wave to its peak.

She was right. It was easy. For her. Pete finally struggled aboard.

"I'll be right back," Dan said leaving Pete and Kate alone on the deck.

"I can't believe you've been coming up all these years and have never sailed," Kate began.

"Well, I guess it's just not something you do if you don't have a sailboat," Pete explained.

"So, besides fishing, what do you do?"

"Oh, I don't know. Read. Hike. Shoot BB's. I play catch with my dad and go to town with my sister. We play cards at night and make popcorn. My mom and I do jigsaw puzzles on rainy days, and we play Scrabble. Not much."

The two stared out toward Elliot Bay.

"It's funny," Kate remarked eventually. "We've been on the same side of this island for ten summers and never met."

"Well, I'm glad we have now," Pete added bashfully. "I'm really anxious to learn how to sail. Is it hard?"

Kate paused. "No, it's easy." She and Dan had sailed since they were born, it seemed. "And it's like nothing else in the world, Pete. You'll love it."

2:05 p.m.

Harold Geetings closed his cabin door and checked the shutters to make sure no one snooping around could see inside. He had come with Fats and Joey two nights before but, because of the torrential downpour all day yesterday, he couldn't get into the post office until today. Fats and Cahill both came to drop him off but had to stay at his cabin for the last two nights. That made him nervous. They weren't used to the Snows. They didn't know how quiet it could get, how sounds could carry across the water. And they argued incessantly. It was a good thing the place was double insulated or everyone in the Snows could have heard them.

He didn't want to leave them alone but he had to get into town. The extra delivery from New York had been due yesterday. Leaving counterfeit paper sitting around at the post office wasn't safe. Someone might get curious and do a little postal inspecting. He was already sure that the postmaster, Archie Visnaw, suspected something. He'd have a hard time explaining all the books and their blank sheets of paper. Especially if someone noticed the tiny red and blue threads in them.

The old man turned from his cottage and walked along the shoreline of his island. He picked up a stone and threw it as hard as he could in the exact direction of Mackinac Island seventeen miles beyond. He aimed it as though, by hitting it, he might sink it. He cursed to himself as the stone arched over the reeds toward Reif's Point. "I've worked all my life to get a book published. All my worthless life. Now, everything's so tangled up, I can't even think."

The stone splashed into the water just beyond the reeds. He walked out onto his dock and turned to the old wooden outboard tied to the left side of the pier. On the other side bobbed the Italian built, three hundred horsepower speedboat. Fats insisted they buy it so they could make their midnight crossings from the Snows to Mackinac Island undetected. But they had to keep it a secret, not an easy assignment in the Snows where boats were everyone's passion.

Harold sat in the stern of his old outboard and pulled the starting cord. The tiny motor putt-putted softly away from the little island. He eased her through the winding passage and into Elliot Bay. He loved this boat. He loved this island. He loved the Snows and all the people who lived here. It was as perfect a place as there was in this mixed-up world.

He looked across the lake at all the cottages. Years ago he had known every person in every one of them. And the two hotels sitting across the bay from each other. What wonderful places they were when he was young. A hundred stories flashed through Harold's mind. They were marvelous stories. He had written complete novels about each of his closest friends, Averill Morrison, Russell Patrick, Arlouine Henny, Frances Wirtle, Richard Eberline, Bob Blome. He had labored over each manuscript for months, sometimes years hoping to present a published book to each of them and tell them, "Here, this is for you. This is how special you are and how much you mean to me."

But every one was rejected. All the plot lines. All the re-writes. All the submissions. The publishers weren't interested in the true lives of genuinely nice people anymore. All they wanted was violence and scandalous behavior. Well, Harold was one writer who would never give in. The literary world would, one day, awaken to the fact that the public was tired of such trash. And when it did, Harold would be ready with volumes of great material. Unfortunately for Harold, he'd run out of money first. He was forced to deal with such lowlife as Fats FitzRoberts just to stay alive.

2:12 p.m.

Pete and Kate gazed out past the bow of the *Griffin* toward Elliot Bay. "Look, Kate," he said pointing. "There's Mr. Geetings."

"If it is, where's his new speedboat?" Kate asked.

"I don't know, but if he keeps coming this way and goes into town, we'll have plenty of time to explore his island."

"Ahoy, there," Eddie bellowed as he and Dan rowed up in the dinghy. "Come now, me hearties. You'll be standin' straight and tall as your cap'n boards his vessel, right enough, or I'll have ye walk the plank, I will."

Dan followed in his best Long John Silver brogue, "Stand aside for the cap'n. Oh, you are a scurvy lot, to be sure. Avast, and ahoy, lubbers."

The two pirates hopped aboard. Dan quickly noticed Pete and Kate's somber expressions. "Why so serious?" he asked, dropping the buccaneer's dialect. "Summer hasn't been cancelled, has it?"

"Look over there," Kate said, nodding toward Mr. Geetings as his boat approached the Islington Point buoy.

2:12 p.m.

Harold's outboard slowly made its way into Cedarville Channel. Up ahead along Cincinnati Row, there was the usual assortment of resort activity. Harold would have to keep an eye out for those pesky kids on the mahogany sailboat starting out from the red double boathouse. It seemed like they were forever getting in his way lately. Or maybe he just noticed it more now.

He didn't mind that he no longer took part in the resort activities. He just wanted to write. No one seemed to understand that. He hated to dwell on misfortune. He never had before, even with all the years of rejection slips. But this was different.

"How am I going to get out of this mess?" Harold muttered to himself. "I'm in as deep as Fats now. And that little banty rooster, Joey Cahill, he's going to get us thrown in jail before the summer is out. If we can just make it until September without getting caught I'll be done with Fats and his gangster friends forever. I'll have enough money to write anything I want, wherever I want, for the rest of my life."

2:13 p.m.

"Hurry, Eddie, unlock the cabin," Kate urged.

"Och, no, m'lassie. You'll not be orderin' this ol' cap'n around, or soon you'll be walkin' the plank, sure you will," the big, dark-haired Eddie growled with a playful sneer on his lips. He unlocked the cabin door, went below, and hauled out two large, white bags, several thin, wooden sticks, and yards of 3/8 inch hemp line.

"Stand aside, lubber," Eddie grinned at Pete squinting his left eye. "Me and me mates'll 'ave this 'ere ship rigged and flyin' afore ye can blink yer e'e, sure enough, heh, heh, don't y'know, or me name's not Eddie the Turk."

"Aye," Dan snorted, "but ye can make your landlubbin' paws of some use a'stuffin' these 'ere battens in yon main's'l, like so, heh, heh." He nimbly poked a stave into a long, slim pocket sewn into the sail and tucked the end back out of sight. "You'll be observin' they're of different lengths, right enough, so mind ye of that, to be sure."

Pete hadn't even cast off and sailing was already more fun than he could have imagined. He glanced up and saw Mr. Geetings directly across the channel staring dead ahead.

"H'ist the main, matey," Eddie called to Dan. "Cast the mooring line, lassie," he said to Kate, and she detached the *Griffin* from its mooring ball.

They were away, sure enough, heh, heh, right they were, and Pete's first sailing adventure was about to begin.

CHAPTER 11
MYSTERY ISLAND

2:20 p.m.

A soft, westerly breeze in the channel brought the *Griffin* across the bow of Mr. Geetings' slow moving outboard. They had each encountered the old man dozens of times over the summers and been able to ignore him with unflagging ease. Now he was the focus of their every thought. There he was, not twenty yards off their port bow, staring grimly ahead wearing a long black coat and a weathered skipper's hat.

Eddie guided the *Griffin* toward the Islington Hotel completing the circle around the old man's boat. The wind slowly filled the mainsail, and the mahogany sloop gracefully headed down Cedarville Channel.

Once past the Islington buoy, the unsheltered wind roared over the tops of the trees and caught hold of the *Griffin's* jib and main sails.

Eddie, Dan, and Kate had come into this bay a thousand times. They knew exactly how the boat would be affected and casually prepared themselves to lean out to the windward by slipping their feet into the hiking straps as they neared the end of Cedarville Channel.

Pete, quite understandably, did not. As the strong breeze hit the sails, the *Griffin* instantly went from one to eight knots and heeled over on a 45-degree angle. Pete immediately lost his balance and flew on his face. He knew for a fact that the boat was out of control and would sink in a minute. All he could see was a wall of water where the deck had been moments before. Whatever Pete had envisioned as being be so terrific about sailing was very quickly shrouded by the imminent prospect of death. As he was about to be washed overboard, he grabbed a guy wire and held on for dear life. For the moment, he was safe.

He next thought of his friends who probably had not been so lucky. He spun his head to the left looking behind the boat for one or more of them waving their arms in distress, but there was no sign of any of them. Perhaps they had already drowned. Frantically, Pete turned his head to the starboard.

There they were, all three of them eagerly leaning way out over the side urging their small vessel on to even greater speeds. Eddie was holding the tiller and watching the jib. Dan was checking the telltale at the top of the mast. And Kate. Kate was arching her back way out over the starboard side facing the sun. Her eyes were closed and a smile of intense pleasure played on her lips.

Pete was, at once, relieved for their safety but embarrassed for his unsailorlike conduct. Finally, Kate opened her eyes and noticed that her new friend was, for some inexplicable reason, grovelling along the deck.

"Come on, Pete," she laughed, "we can't get any hull speed with you on the port. Here, sit with me. I'll show you how it's done. Just tuck your feet in this strap and lean out over the side. It's easy."

Right, Pete thought. *Maybe in another lifetime.*

Eddie kept a straight course almost all the way to Reif's Point. "Ready about!" he announced.

Ready about? Pete thought. *Ready to about what? Or maybe it's short for What's about ready? Probably just another bizarre, Cincinnati expression.* He'd figure it out later. His main concern at the moment was to regain some dignity. He glanced around and was heartened by the momentary decline in the speed of the boat. He sat up straight smiling calmly at Kate as she and Dan scrambled to grab some ropes.

"Hard alee!" Eddie ordered as he pushed the tiller way over to the left.

Hard alee? Pete wondered. *What is THAT all about? Maybe he meant Heartily.*

"Mind the boom, Pete!" Dan hollered.

There was a touch of urgency in Dan's tone and the term *boom*, perhaps, should have been a tip-off to the consequences for not immediately *minding* it, but Pete was trying very hard to appear cool, calm, and composed.

Out of the corner of his left eye, however, he caught a glimpse of a rapidly approaching white wall. Attached to its base was a thick, shiny, brown pole coming toward his head at an incredible rate of speed.

Kate screamed, "Duck!"

Pete understood *Duck* and instantly dropped his head. But evidently not instantly enough. A crash exploded in his brain and tiny lights flashed behind his eyes. They twinkled brightly and then, slowly, flickered out.

—

Gradually, Pete became aware of a flapping sound. The sun penetrated his closed eyes and cast a golden tint to what little consciousness he was able to muster.

"Is he dead?"

"I don't know. He got whacked pretty hard."

"You guys should have been going slower. You could have gone into Sheppard Bay for awhile to show him what to do. If he's dead, I'll never forgive either of you."

Pete slowly realized where he was and why.

"He's moving," Kate said. "Pete. Are you okay?"

Pete opened his eyes and the sun shot directly to the center of his brain. The pain was excruciating.

"Oh, Pete," Kate said softly, "I was so scared. Don't ever do that again."

It wasn't something Pete had consciously tried to do in the first place, but he appreciated her concern. "I'm all right, I guess," he said rubbing the top of his head. He sat up and looked out to survey the boat's location and found that it was slowly drifting into the shallow bay behind Mr. Geetings' island. "How much time do we have?" Pete asked.

"Oh, we still have an hour or so," Dan replied. "Are you sure you're up to this? You've got quite a knot up there."

"Yeah, I'm okay. Really," Pete said more to reassure himself than his friends. He knew how much this spying mission meant to Kate, and he certainly didn't want to disappoint her.

"Okay," Eddie said as he eased the tiller off dead center. The flapping sound stopped as the sails filled and the *Griffin* moved ahead. "I've never been back here before," Eddie continued. "Does anyone have any idea what kind of water we're in?"

"It's plenty deep but huge boulders are everywhere," Pete said. "Mr. Geetings has a winding channel cut into the reeds where he docks his boat. I've never gone in there, though. My mom told me years ago never to bother him."

The tall green reeds completely surrounded the island and were dense enough to keep anyone from seeing any more than Mr. Geetings' cabin roof. It was a perfect hideout.

"Okay, let's go in," Eddie directed. "Dan, lean out over the bow and watch for rocks. Kate, be ready to crank up the centerboard. And Pete . . . ?"

"What, Eddie?" Pete asked anxiously.

"Do me a big favor and mind the boom," Eddie grinned.

———

Once in the channel the four sailors were completely hidden both from the island in front of them and the open water off their stern. Pete began to hear the muffled hum of a machine and, as the *Griffin* rounded the last cut in the reed bed, a dock appeared to the left of the cabin. Pete had always assumed that the old man's cottage was a decrepit, old shack. It was, in fact, a small, but beautifully built summer home.

"Over there!" Kate said pointing to the dock.

On the far side was the shining black hull of a speedboat bobbing gently in the water.

The *Griffin's* shallow draft keel ground to a halt on the sand and pebble beach.

"I'm going ashore," Dan said. "Anyone with me?"

Pete welcomed the opportunity to stand on firm soil. "I'm right behind you, Dan."

Dan hurried over to the speedboat. Pete went the other way to get a closer look at the cottage. As he drew near, he was surprised to hear voices. He dropped to his knees behind a bush. As he listened, he noticed a small, yellowed envelope laying on the rocks. Without thinking, he picked it up and stuffed it in his hip pocket. Suddenly, he became aware of footsteps approaching from behind. He spun his head apprehensively, ready to bolt. It was Dan. Relieved, Pete put a finger up to his lips and motioned him to come to his side.

"Listen," Pete whispered. "What do you hear?"

Dan paused, "A machine. Maybe a generator."

The two knelt motionless. "Yeah, I guess it could be," Pete agreed. "But it sounds to me like a printing press."

"A printing press?"

"Yeah. Like they used for my school newspaper. But that's not all. A minute ago, I heard voices."

Kate had been watching from the *Griffin* and couldn't take the intrigue any longer. She jumped ship joining Pete and Dan.

"What's going on?" she whispered.

"There!" Pete said. "Did you hear that? It sounds far away, but it can't be. And it's no radio."

"It's two men," Dan said. "And it sounds like they're arguing. I've got a feeling we'd better get out of here. Come on, let's go."

He turned and, bending low, ran for the sailboat. Pete and Kate followed less than a step behind. Eddie had stayed aboard, holding the *Griffin* off shore with a small paddle. At the sight of his landing party slinking across the island toward him, he nosed the bow up to the shore. The three boarded quickly with Dan shoving off.

"Ready about. Keep your head down, Pete," Eddie warned. "Hard alee." He spun the rudder and the main sail filled sending the boom flying over the tops of their heads. The *Griffin* slipped into the narrow channel. Behind them, back on the island, a door slammed. All four sailors spun around but could see only a wall of tall, green reeds.

"Pop the jib, Dan," Eddie ordered. "We'll make for Connors Point."

Soon, the *Griffin* was far out into Elliot Bay with four wide-eyed sailors aboard, their minds racing at speeds that would challenge the mysterious black-hulled boat they'd just left on the tiny, green island.

CHAPTER 12
THE CLUES

3:00 p.m.

Pete became a sailor that afternoon for as good a reason as any: blind terror. Kate showed him how to hook his feet into the hiking straps, and he launched himself backwards over the starboard gunwale. The *Griffin* flew out from the writer's island toward Connors Point. They didn't drop sail or even speak to one another until they came to Sheppard Bay.

Even there, in the calm, secluded privacy of the cedar tree-lined shore, the four spoke only in hushed tones. No more "Me hearties" this or "To be sure" that.

They talked in dead earnest of what they had seen and heard: the mysterious speedboat, the printing press, the shuttered cabin, the voices, the argument. Had the *Griffin* been seen in her retreat? Who was on the old man's island, anyway?

As each point was discussed, the crew became more and more restless. Had their imaginations taken over? An hour passed. Dan glanced up. He saw a small motorboat sliding silently out of Cedarville Channel, past the Islington buoy into Elliot Bay. He didn't have to look twice to know who it was. He nodded in that direction and all four watched as Mr. Geetings' boat inched its way toward the tiny island they had just fled. Approaching the reeds, it veered to the left.

"Does the bow look like it's riding low?" Eddie asked.

"It sure does," Pete responded. "I'll bet he's got another load of boxes from the post office." That reminded him. From his left hip pocket he withdrew the envelope he had found on the island.

"Where'd you get that?" Kate asked.

"Just outside Mr. Geetings' cabin," Pete replied.

As Pete unfolded it, he saw only one word scrawled in streaked ink across the front. "*Fats.*"

"What's in it, Pete?" Eddie asked.

The back flap was unsealed. Pete opened it.

"It's empty," he replied. "It's nothing."

"Hardly," Dan said softly. "I think it tells us a lot."

"Come on," Eddie said. "It's just an old envelope that washed up on shore. It doesn't mean a thing."

"Not from where Pete found it," Dan reasoned. "He was twenty feet from the beach so it couldn't possibly have washed up on that part of the shore. Besides, if it had been in the water for any time at all, the writing would be all smeared. That, and I think I know who Fats is."

"All right, Sherlock," Eddie said sarcastically. "Who's Fats?"

"It may be just a hunch," Dan replied, "but sup-

66

pose we all tell everything we know. When we're done, see if you don't think I'm right."

"You mean, we all know who Fats is?" Pete asked.

"You might not, Pete," Dan nodded, "but I believe the rest of us know him all too well."

"All right, Dan," Eddie said, leaning into the center of the four. "Let's hear it."

"Okay," Dan began. "Remember our midnight sail over to Mackinac Island last year? We arrived at about one a.m. and docked at the closest slip on the east end of the pier. It was the very slip that we saw Mr. Geetings pulling out of last week. Anyway, we went ashore, stayed the night at Aunt and Uncle's place, came down the next morning, and the *Griffin* had been moved. In its place was a long, low boat of some kind that was completely covered with a black tarp. The *Griffin* was docked in the next slip over."

"That's right," Eddie said. "We asked the dockhand on duty, a college guy named Steve, how the *Griffin* got moved."

"Yes," Kate added, "Steve said that's where it was when he came on duty at six a.m. Dan asked Steve if we could talk to the head dockmaster. He told us to come back at two that afternoon."

Pete interrupted, "Why did you care so much that the *Griffin* had been moved?"

"For one thing, Pete," Eddie replied, "it's illegal. Maritime law says that a boat can't be moved in harbor without the captain's permission. Someone had untied the *Griffin* so that the speedboat could be docked in that particular slip."

"But why?" Pete asked, still confused.

"It didn't make any sense to me then, either, Pete," Dan replied, "but my guess now is that Mr.

Geetings uses that boat to smuggle counterfeit money from the Snows to Mackinac. He does it at night so no one ever sees the boat move. If he can keep it covered and in that same slip all summer, eventually no one would even notice it. Anyway, we went back to the dock at two that afternoon and met a great big guy with *Gerald* on his name tag. We showed him where we docked. He laughed at us and said that the speedboat hadn't been out all summer. He said some rich guy owned it and he hardly ever used it. Then he told us to get lost.

"Now," Dan said slowly, "do either of you remember what one of the yachtsmen called `Gerald' when he yelled out to him?"

"Yes!" Kate said. "I remember it now as plain as day. He called out, `Hey, Fats!'"

"That's right," Dan said. "And I think the envelope Pete found today belonged to Gerald, or Fats, Mackinac Island's head dockmaster. Fats, at the very least, is covering for Harold Geetings. He might even be behind the whole operation."

They all sat in silence. The *Griffin* bounced softly in the light breeze.

"It's possible, Dan," Eddie entered thoughtfully. His concerned expression slowly broke into a brawny smile. "I guess we'll just have to sail over to Mackinac to find out."

"Our parents probably won't let us go right away," Dan said, "but if we start campaigning now, we may be able to go in a week or so."

"In the meantime," Kate added, "we can do some snooping around town to find out what's in those boxes he's getting from the post office and carting out to his island."

Eddie stood up. "All hands on deck. This is your cap'n speakin'. Make ready to set the mains'l, lad. You there, lassie, h'ist the jib. Cabin boy, prepare to get ready to mind the boom, pretty soon, and at your convenience, of course, don't ye know."

The *Griffin* made her way out of Sheppard Bay and was soon heeling over at 45 degrees with her captain and three crewmen straining to wind'ard catching every breath of air the Snows could offer. Eddie steered a course through Elliot Bay to the second red double boathouse in Cincinnati Row.

"Drop the jib, Dan," Eddie called out. "Let off on the main, Kate. Snap a line to the ball, Pete. There we are. And what a fine, wee sail it was, me hearties, to be sure, heh, heh."

Dan and Kate's mother came down to the boathouse wearing a yellow gingham dress and matching sun bonnet.

"Dinner will be served in half an hour," she called out. "Clean up and change your clothes. Peter, you're welcome to join us."

Clothes changed? For dinner? Pete had never changed his clothes for dinner in his life. Besides he didn't have anything that would look any different than the blue jeans and white tee-shirt he was already wearing. His three friends were already overdressed for any occasion that he would ever care to encounter. Now they were going to go into their cottage and change into better clothes? And for what? To eat? These kids had to put up with an awful lot just to get through a day around here.

"I'd better hightail it on home, ma'am," Pete called back. *In the meantime*, he thought, *I'm overdue for some required reading. And, if I know my mom at all, it's sitting right on top of my stack of comics.*

"Some other time, then, Peter."

"You bet," he waved. "See y'round."

He trotted down the wide, wooden dock to shore and disappeared onto the path behind the trees leading to his cottage. He ran full speed all the way past the turreted armed guards who, he could distinctly hear, threw rounds of ammunition into their rifle chambers every time he slowed his pace. He found the notched cedar trees that marked the tunnel and ducked into the passage coming out in the sunny, open area of the Elliot Hotel front lawn. He jogged easily along the narrow, dusty pathway in front of the Elliot Row cabins. In another minute, he was in his living room, the front screen door slapping behind him.

"Wash up. Dinner's almost ready," his mother said.

Pete headed over to his stack of comics. There it was, right on top, *Emily Post's Etiquette For Teens*.

His mom peeked into the living room from the kitchen. Seeing Pete reach for his favorite reading materials, she quickly admonished, "No time for comics, Pete. Help your sister set the table."

(caderville Channel)

CHAPTER 13
SPIED

6:00 p.m.

The usual scurrying around just before dinner made conversation impossible in the Jenkins' kitchen. Cara set the table. Pete was in charge of getting the milk out of the ice box and filling two rubber drinking cups. He then put a stack of sliced bread on a small plate, got the butter dish from the ice box and set them in the center of the table.

Mr. Jenkins gave the fish a final turn in the frying pan then lifted the fillets onto the old, china platter. Pete's mom poured the coffee, ladled out the fried potatoes, and sliced several tomatoes and carrots onto a serving dish.

Somehow, they all managed to sit down at the same time.

"Well, Pete," his mom said, "what did you do all day?"

She had asked him that very question at dinnertime every summer day for as long as Pete could remember. He had always provided pretty much the same answer: "Well, I went fishing at such-and-such dock and caught so many of this kind of fish." This summer, though, all of that had changed. Since Pete had met his new friends, he had been going special places, doing special things, and meeting special people. He had plenty to talk about.

Tonight was no different. Except for just one thing. This evening, for the first time ever, Pete had to hold back. He slowed his eating pace trying to decide how much of his day's activities he could divulge. He really wanted to explain what he and his friends suspected about Mr. Geetings and what they had seen on the old man's island. But he knew he'd been forbidden from even being there. He also wanted to begin campaigning for the Mackinac Island trip. He sat in his chair struggling with how to answer his mom's question.

"I learned how to sail," he said rubbing the bump on the top of his head. "We went out on Eddie Terkel's boat. They showed me how to tack, and jibe, and come about, and all sorts of stuff. They've asked me to sail with them over to Mackinac Island sometime, maybe in a couple of weeks. Dan and Kate have relatives over there. Can I go?"

"Oh, Pete, I don't know," his mom replied. "Your dad and I will have to talk it over. I'm not very comfortable with you out on the open water, especially if you're depending on the wind to get you all the way to Mackinac Island and back. We'll see."

That did it. "We'll see," with his mom, meant "In a pig's eye." Pete had better hold off on the news about Mr. Geetings' island for another day.

"What does Eddie's sailboat look like?" Cara asked, casually pawing at a bite of sliced potato with her fork.

72

"It's a real beaut, Cara," Pete replied. "You know when we're at the end of Cincinnati Row on our way to town? It's the dark, mahogany one moored in front of the red double boathouse. It really flies with a good wind."

"Then that was you I saw as I was coming back from Bosely Channel. You and your friends were just going into Mr. Geetings' island," Cara said triumphantly. "I just knew it. What were you doing over there?"

The cat was out of the bag now. *Thanks, Cara,* Pete thought. The discussion went on well past dishwashing and, for once, the topic of conversation wasn't the raccoons and deer coming up to feast on the Jenkins' leftovers.

"Look, Pete," his dad said. "I don't care what you thought you saw and heard on that island, Harold Geetings is no crook. He's not doing anything over there but minding his own business, which, if you want to continue to visit your new friends, you will do, as well."

"Okay," Pete promised, "I'll never bother Mr. Geetings at his island again."

Cara looked warily at her little brother.

———

That night Pete lay awake in his bunk adding up all the circumstances.

"Cara?" he whispered toward his sister's bed.

"What, Pete?" she whispered back.

"Don't you believe me?" Pete asked.

"No."

"But we heard voices. People arguing. We saw the speedboat and heard a printing press. The place was shut up tighter than Fort Knox. Don't you see? It all points to Mr. Geetings making counterfeit money over there, and he's probably doing it this very minute."

"No, he is not, Pete," Cara said, measuring her words. "What you kids saw and heard today can all be explained. Mr. Geetings is a writer. He likes to work at night. He has a generator to run his lights so he can write after dark. Because he works late, he doesn't like to be awakened by the sun in the morning, so he keeps his shutters closed. He has a radio. While he's away, he leaves it on to keep intruders, little snoops like you, from poking around his cabin. Today, you and your crimestopper friends sneaked onto his island, heard the radio, probably *Gangbusters*, and raced away with your imaginations in full gear. As you were leaving, the wind just happened to blow open a shutter and it slammed shut. That's all.

"Writers, Pete, are eccentric. They're nuttier than pecan pies. And he's rich. They all are. He has a speedboat that he uses for long trips, perhaps to Mackinac Island, but he likes his old outboard. The only thing strange going on over there is in your minds. Pete, give it a rest. Leave the old man alone."

Pete remained silent.

"Did you hear me, Pete?"

That was another infuriating thing about his big sister. She was always right.

"Okay," Pete said.

He lay in his bunk mulling over everything she'd said. He stacked each of her points against what he had seen and heard that afternoon. Before going to sleep, Pete made a decision. *You're wrong, Cara*, Pete thought. *This time you're wrong, and I'm going to prove it.*

Loading the shipment

CHAPTER 14
GOOD DEED DAY

Thursday, June 26   2:30 p.m.

A week and a half later as Pete and Cara took the *Flossy* into town for their daily errands, Pete noticed that Danny's red and white outboard was not at his boathouse. *I'll bet they're in town at the Bon Air,* he thought.

"You get the mail, Pete," Cara said as they tied up at the city dock. "I'll start the groceries. Meet me inside at Hossack's."

Pete ran up to the post office and as he reached for the knob to go in, the door flew open. Two big boxes charged out toward him followed by Mr. Geetings. As Pete spun out of the way, he tripped and fell in the dirt next to the door.

"Blasted kids. They're everywhere," Harold Geetings cursed as he blustered by.

Pete picked himself up, quickly realizing this might be his chance to learn something.

"Are you okay, Pete?" Archie Visnaw asked from behind his counter.

"Yeah, I guess," Pete said brushing himself off. "Say, what's with that old guy? He almost knocked my mom over two weeks ago coming out of here."

"Oh, that's Mr. Geetings. He's a writer," Mr. Visnaw said, as if that would explain everything. "Word around town is that he wrote a novel or something and now he's having the books shipped here. It's been going on for over a year. Nobody's actually seen a copy of it but he's been getting lots of big boxes, all postmarked from New York."

Mr. Visnaw disappeared momentarily into the back room to get the Jenkins' mail. He returned with the *Saginaw News* and a few letters addressed to Pete's parents. Pete turned and hurried out the door making a beeline past Hossack's to the Bon Air. He quickly found his three friends and pulled up a chair from a nearby table.

"I can only stay for a minute," Pete said, "but guess who I just ran into. Mr. Geetings and two big boxes."

"You just saw him?" Kate asked.

"Maybe we can catch him before he loads his boat," Dan said pushing his chair back. "Let's go."

In a flash, all four bolted out of the Bon Air and headed toward the dock. There he was, almost to the very end of the pier.

"You three go ahead," Pete said. "If he sees me, he'll know something's up."

Pete stopped at the side of Hossack's while Eddie led the way. They came up to within thirty feet of the old man and then slowed to a casual trot. Kate took the lead and approached Mr. Geetings from behind.

"Hi, mister," she said cheerfully.

"Hi, yourself," the grizzled old man grumbled back setting the cardboard cases next to his boat.

76

"Do you need any help with those boxes?" she asked politely. "Today is Good Deed Day' at our club and we get points for helping people."

Mr. Geetings turned and glared at the three shiny-faced, teenagers. He wasn't just an old man. He was a big, strong, mean-looking, old man. He had wide, square shoulders. Deep furrows creased his forehead. He wore a thick, black beard and towered over all three. It didn't look as if he had an ounce of fat anywhere under his long, black overcoat.

"'Good Deed Day,' is it?" he growled, a smile escaping from behind his beard. "Well, they are heavy. Books, you know. You boys hand me one box at a time. Mind you, be careful." He stepped cat-like into the center of his long, narrow boat and turned to take the first carton.

Kate stood to the side trying to memorize every detail on the packages. "Looks like you've got a lot of reading to do, mister," she said.

"It would seem so," he replied. "Okay, boys, careful now."

Dan and Eddie together strained to pick up one box. The boys glanced at each other as each realized how strong the old coot must be to have carried both boxes at once. Mr. Geetings set the first one in the bow and the second in the center of the boat.

"Thanks, mister," Kate piped up, after both were safely aboard. "Maybe we can help you again another day." She started down the dock, leaving Dan and Eddie to offer their own good-byes.

———

"Quiet," she said as they caught up with her by Hossack's back door. Pete came out from behind the storage area and all four gathered in a huddle. "Where's a pencil?"

77

Dan quickly found one and Kate put it to use on a Bon Air napkin.

Verity Press & Paper
2000 Jackson Avenue
New York, 27, New York

"Okay," she said. "That's the return address."

"What do we do with that?" Eddie asked.

"Hey, I don't know," Kate replied. "What did you guys get?"

"Scared," Dan and Eddie looked up and mumbled to each other.

"Okay," Kate huffed, "I say we go to the post office and find out what we can about what I got."

"I hope we find out that he's carrying nothing more than what he says he is," Dan said.

"That's right," Eddie echoed, "I'd never want to tangle with that old guy."

Pete hoped for the first time ever that his sister was right. He was almost willing to forget the whole adventure. Almost. Except for just one thing . . .

"Okay, guys," Kate chirped, tossing back her long blond hair and smiling excitedly. "We've got work to do." Pete was absolutely mesmerized by her.

"I've got to get back to Hossack's," Pete said to his three friends as they headed toward the post office. "My sister will think I fell in."

"Oh, Pete," Dan called out as Pete reached the back door of the general store. "Tomorrow we're going over to Sandy Beach on the *Escape*. You're invited. Meet us at our place at noon if you want to join us. Bring your bathing suit."

Pete just stood and stared as his friends turned toward the post office. *The Escape? Holy cow!*

The *Escape* was an awesome cabin cruiser that took up the entire Cedarville Channel when it came to the Snows each year. He didn't know who owned it but it was often tied up at the green, triple-boathouse next to Dan and Eddie's. To Pete, the *Escape* was not so much someone's possession as it was a being of its own—a beautiful, graceful, living entity. He would never think of boarding her, much less going out for an afternoon's excursion.

He stood in a trance as he watched his friends disappear into the post office. Finally he remembered he was supposed to be helping his sister. He spun on his heels and charged directly into a large, cardboard box of groceries.

"And here I'd thought you'd forgotten me," Cara grumbled as she shoved the box further into Pete's chest. "We'll have to skip the Bon Air today in order to get this milk home before it turns to cottage cheese. You've been a big help."

Pete crammed the mail into the top of the grocery box and hurried to catch up.

His mind was racing. What would he do? Who would he meet? He couldn't wait to get home to tell his mom and dad. He'd need to get started right away on the Emily Post book.

The Escape

CHAPTER 15
SOCIAL GRACES

4:00 p.m.

When Pete told Cara his news as they walked down the dock to the *Flossy*, she stopped in her tracks. "You're going to a picnic on the *Escape*?" she asked. "So, what will you wear for your day's ensemble, Mr. Fashion, your fishing clothes?"

Pete hadn't thought about that. He figured he had enough to do memorizing the manners book between then and the next morning. But as Cara drove the *Flossy* past Cincinnati Row, he acknowledged the obvious. He could learn everything there was to know about etiquette, but unless he dressed the part, he would still look and feel like a hayseed. He would be introduced to probably a hundred people who, clothed in proper yachting attire, would take one look at him and ask, "Who invited the waif?" He'd not only be an embarrassment to himself, but to his friends, as well.

Returning to the cottage, however, Pete barely mentioned the *Escape* to his parents and his mom said, "Well, Pete, you can't very well go places and expect to meet people on equal terms if you insist on wearing fishing clothes all your life. Come on. Let's go into town. We'll just count this as an early back-to-school shopping trip."

There was only one place in all the Les Cheneaux Islands to buy clothes: Hossack's General Store where Pete and Cara bought groceries every day. Pete had never had the occasion to visit the back where the dry goods were kept. The ancient wooden floors creaked and groaned as he and his mom walked along the aisles. They picked out two pairs of shorts, a couple shirts, and a boat-neck sweater—stuff like Dan and Eddie always had on. Pete also had noticed that they always wore those soft, brown leather, boating shoes, something he'd never even seen back in Saginaw. He looked down at his worn-out, black, basketball shoes. They looked pretty shabby.

His mom said, "Look over here, Pete. Wouldn't you like a pair of these nice, rubber soled, leather moccasins?"

How does she do that? Pete wondered.

———

In less than an hour, they were back aboard the *Flossy* heading out of Cedarville Bay. Pete was feeling like a million bucks. As they buzzed along Cincinnati Row he got to thinking how his summers in the Snows had been so simple for so long. Now, everything was different. Two weeks ago the only decision he had to make was whether to use a red and white Dardevle with a *silver* back or a red and white Dardevle with a *copper* back. Being with his new friends was fun and everything, but it might be nice to go fishing once again with nothing more on his mind than his hat.

When they returned to their cottage, Pete pulled down the Emily Post book from its place atop the stack of comics and opened it to the table of contents.

"Here, Pete," Averill Jenkins said pointing to a line in the center of the page. "'Social Pleasantries'—Start with this chapter and then we'll go over any questions you have. I'll fix dinner."

Pete poured over the material with new interest. He learned the proper ways to say hello and good-bye, two subjects he'd never even thought about before. *C'mon,* he thought. *How hard can this be?* He discovered, however, that "Hi, how y'doin'," and "S'long, see y'round," would hardly be appropriate aboard the *Escape*. Greeting people and introducing friends required special phrases that were totally foreign to him.

Realizing he needed some practical application, Pete moved his study area to the privacy of his bedroom and worked in front of his sister's full length mirror next to the vanity table. He was concentrating on the proper expressions to use if introduced to the Princess of England, who he imagined looked remarkably like Kate, when his sister, Cara, the Toad Duchess of Transylvania, waltzed casually through his bedroom's curtained doorway. She caught him in a perfect genuflect at the feet of the charming and lovely, kerosene lantern. She caustically remarked, "Extending our circle of friends, Petey-wetey?"

In a flash, she whirled out of Buckingham Palace's Great Chamber for the safety of the Jenkins' cottage living room, leaving Pete alone with Princess Nightlight.

If nothing else, Pete had to admire his sister's cat-like reflexes. By all rights, she should be wearing in the center of her back the book he now held scrunched in his left hand.

Undeterred, Pete launched into the "Table Manners" and the "Yacht Parties" chapters. The more he learned, the more he realized he didn't stand a chance. Some of the rules were so strange that he didn't think he'd ever be able to accomplish any of them without looking and sounding like a complete Bozo.

When his mom called in to see how he was faring, Pete came out to the living room and asked her about feeling so out of place.

"Be yourself, Pete," she said. "This book is simply a guide to show people you respect them. Each of the rules is based on treating others as you would like to be treated. Keep that in mind and your actions will speak louder than words."

"Yeah, I guess so," Pete said. "It just seems like there's so much to learn. Say, I've got an idea. How about we go over all the table manner stuff at dinner tonight?"

"Why, Pete," Mrs. Jenkins said, standing back in mock astonishment, "I never thought I'd see the day. This Kate of yours must be quite the young lady."

"Aw, Mom, now don't you start on me. One in the family's enough."

"All right, Pete. I'll quiz you at dinner tonight. In the meantime, I'm sure your father could use some help down at the lake."

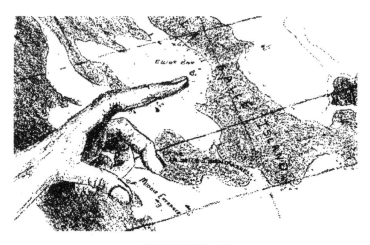

CHAPTER 16
THE CHART

Friday, June 27 11:45 a.m.

Pete awakened the next morning and by a quarter to twelve closed his book and put on his new clothes. He guessed he'd crammed as much etiquette into his head as would fit. "Mom," he called into the kitchen. "I'm going now."

The front screen slapped shut and he was on the path to the Elliot Hotel. He darted through the tunnel and raced along Cincinnati Row never looking up at the summer homes on his right. In ten minutes he'd run the mile to Kate and Dan's place, gone up the cottage steps, and knocked on the door.

"Come on in," Kate smiled. "Nice shirt. You're right on time."

"Hello, Pete," Dr. Hinken said, approaching him from the stairway. He was decked out in his beach finery and carried a large wicker picnic basket. "Glad you could come, Pete," he smiled. "You must be good luck. This is the first time in ages we've held the Sandy Beach picnic on the day it was scheduled."

"Uh, thank you, sir. I'm sure looking forward to it. I've never been on a boat like the *Escape*."

"All right, everyone," Mrs. Hinken said, "I think we're ready."

The entourage headed for the front door and onto the trail leading toward the green triple-boathouse where the luxury cruiser was docked. As they walked onto the wide pier, Pete heard voices coming from inside the *Escape*.

"Permission to board, Bill?" Dr. Hinken called into the darkened glass door of the enormous yacht.

"Come aboard, Dan. We're all below," came a jovial response.

Pete followed Kate as she stepped onto the deck and then down a wide companionway into the main salon. It was as plush a room as Pete had ever seen. There, probably twenty-five people were engaged in animated chatter. Pete was meeting people in such bewildering numbers that he began to wonder if he might forget his own name. Dan stayed nearby and for that, Pete swore his undying gratitude.

The low drone of the *Escape*'s engines fired, and then, from up top, a booming voice called down,

"All ashore that's going ashore.
Man the lines. We sail at dawn."

It was the voice of authority and yet of good humor sung out as though it were part of an old, traditional chant. It disregarded the obvious fact that the time of day was a little past noon. Several people leaped from their seats and scurried to the upper deck.

"Let's go up top, Pete," Dan said. "We're casting off."

Pete followed Dan to the bow where Dan tossed the shore line onto the dock. The *Escape* backed slowly from the boathouse, then majestically, turned and headed along Cincinnati Row toward Cedarville.

With all the excitement of boarding the *Escape*, Pete suddenly realized that Eddie was missing.

"Oh," Dan said, "Eddie took the *Silver Moon* and will meet us at Sandy Beach to help everyone ashore. People from all over the Snows will be there." Dan sat down on the long, cushioned bench that ran a few feet back from the bow and stretched out casually. Pete joined him and watched the shoreline as the *Escape* passed the Ailes Point buoy across from Cedarville and followed the narrow markers toward Island Number Eight.

Once beyond Cedarville Bay, the captain pushed the RPMs up until the *Escape* was moving at a pretty good clip. Kate came by, and Pete made room for her to sit next to him.

"I've never been over on this side of LaSalle Island," Pete said. "Where are we going?"

Dan and Kate turned and looked at Pete in disbelief.

"How long did you say you've been coming up here?" Kate asked.

"Practically all my life," Pete replied. "I've just never come over here. So, where is Sandy Beach?"

"Follow me," Dan said hopping up, "I'll show you on a chart."

Pete followed Dan and Kate up to the bridge.

"Mr. Terkel," Dan said easily, "I'd like to introduce you to my friend, Pete Jenkins. Pete, this is Mr. William Terkel, Eddie's father and owner of the *Escape*."

Pete's jaw dropped. *Eddie's dad owned the Escape?*

"Well, Pete," Bill Terkel said, "it's nice to have you along."

"Uh, yes sir, it's nice to be had," Pete managed to reply. Then he paused and asked, "You're really Eddie's dad?"

"Yep, all his life. And a pretty good share of mine, as well. Each of these grey hairs comes directly from Eddie's side of the family," he winked.

"Here's the chart, Pete," Dan said, pointing to the detailed nautical map of the Snows. "Sandy Beach is over here beyond Strongs Island. We'll have to anchor out about here," he pointed, "and take the *Silver Moon* into shore. All in all, it's about a half hour run."

Pete had a Lill's Diner place mat pinned up between a couple of two-by-fours in his cottage. It was more of an artist's sketch of the Les Cheneaux Islands than an accurate map. Mr. Terkel's official depth chart, however, showed boathouses, weed beds, rocks, sunken cribs—everything. Pete felt, if he looked hard enough, he might find some big pike or even a muskie in there.

Then Bosely Channel caught his eye. It looked impassable on the chart. Pete looked down in the lower, right hand margin. It read: "Les Cheneaux Islands, 1951." This was 1952. The lake level was at least a foot higher this year and would be safe to get the *Tiny Tin* through easily. Perhaps even the *Flossy* might make it. Then Pete noticed how Mr. Geetings' island was depicted on the chart to be completely surrounded by reeds. Pete knew that was wrong. It didn't show the winding passageway leading to the island, nor did it show the dock where the mystery boat was kept. Pete nudged Dan and pointed to the spot where the *Griffin* had gone ashore.

"That reminds me," Kate said turning away. "Come on."

They left Mr. Terkel on the bridge, made their way through a crowd of people, and found a secluded spot on the foredeck. For the rest of the sail to Sandy Beach, they made their plans for going to Mackinac Island. ___

"Okay, it's agreed," Dan said. "Kate and I will ask our parents today. Eddie's mom and dad have already said he could go. Next, we'll see what we can do about your parents, Pete."

The *Escape's* engines gradually slowed and Bill Terkel's voice crackled over the loudspeaker,

"Everyone off, it's the end of the line.

Gentlemen, please, give a lady your hand."

CHAPTER 17
SANDY BEACH

2:00 p.m.

By two o'clock, Sandy Beach looked like the Les Cheneaux Yacht Club's version of Normandy on D-Day. The attacking marines—the men, women, and children of the Les Cheneaux Islands—were virtually everywhere setting up umbrellas, barbecue pits, and volleyball nets.

Pete was introduced to people from all over the Snows. His softball teammates slapped him on the back and told him how great it was to have beaten the Cedarville squad. Others had heard about his muskie and wanted to know all about that. But beyond the "Nice fish," or "Great play," stage, Pete noticed awkward gulfs in each of their conversations.

Everyone else had been invited because their grandmother or grandfather or aunt or uncle had been part of the festivities for three or four generations, long before they themselves had been born.

He thought back to the softball game and how all the resorters had come to support their team. He suddenly realized that it was not the game they had come to watch. It was simply another social gathering.

Pete had become an associate member of this exclusive circle primarily as the result of two lucky catches, a fish and a softball.

Eventually, Pete drifted away from the beach and found himself on top of a sand dune overlooking the party. As he watched the festivities below, Eddie, Dan, and Kate came up from behind.

"Hey, Pete," Dan said, "Good news. It's on. We'll be taking the *Griffin* and leaving in two days. My father said he'd come down to your place and talk to your parents tomorrow."

"You look a little worried," Eddie said. "You still want to come, don't you?"

"Are you kidding? Sure," Pete said. "But did you tell him why we're really going? About Mr. Geetings, and all?"

"Well, he didn't ask and I guess it slipped my mind," Dan smiled.

"Anyway," Eddie interjected flexing his muscles, "with me around to protect you, what can happen?"

"Oh, you don't have to talk me into it," Pete laughed. "Just my parents. Especially my mom. She doesn't trust any body of water that's over her head."

"We told my father that the main reason we're going is because you've never been to Mackinac," Kate said. "And it's true, sort of. I mean, it's one of the reasons. Oh, Pete, this will be an adventure like none we've every had before."

"Let's get down to the beach," Dan said. "Duke and Moose are starting a volleyball game and we need you on our side. It's us against all the Chicago people."

"Yes," Eddie added. "We've convinced them that your end of the island is just an extension of Cincinnati Row."

"Please?" Pete smiled, raising an eyebrow.

"Now you've got it," Eddie laughed. "Those Chicago kids will never know what hit them."

Rigging the Griffin

CHAPTER 18
THE MEETING

Saturday, June 28 10:00 a.m.

At ten o'clock the next morning, Pete and his mom were sitting on their front porch swing. She was reading her novel and he was studying his *Emily Post.*

Pete also kept one eye on the Elliot dock where he expected, any minute, Dr. Hinken would bring the *Polly Ann* in from along Cedarville Channel. When the Hacker Craft appeared, Pete called inside, "Dad, he's coming!"

Three minutes later Dr. Hinken stepped briskly along the stone path. Howard and Averill Jenkins stood to greet him. They settled into the rocking chairs on the porch, each with a cup of coffee.

"I don't know if you're aware of this," Daniel Hinken began, "but my son and daughter have really enjoyed Pete's company this summer. They say he's learned how to sail quicker than anyone they've ever met. And they'll never forget that day he taught them how to fish. He's become a very welcome addition to our circle of friends.

"When Dan and Kate told me Pete had never been to Mackinac Island, I suggested they take him over in the *Griffin*. Thirty years ago when Eddie's dad, Bill, and I were their age, we used to take her over all the time. She's as seaworthy now as she was then. Kate, Dan, and Eddie grew up on her. Bill and I taught them everything we knew but before long, they were teaching us. We used to accompany them on their excursions until two years ago when they convinced us they could handle any sailing condition that might arise. We even took them on a midnight cruise but all we did was watch.

"They'll be staying with my wife's brother, George Anderson and his wife, Nancy. They have a summer home on the west bluff. They're always happy to have the kids visit, and they're welcome to stay as long as they like. When the kids are there, George calls at nine o'clock every morning and night just to keep us from worrying. Before the kids return to the Snows, George checks with the Coast Guard to make sure the weather conditions will be perfect for the sail."

"Well," Averill Jenkins said, "it sounds more reasonable now than when Pete explained it last night."

"I've never sailed," Howard Jenkins said, "but I know the Great Lakes can be pretty tricky. You're sure Pete won't get in the way?"

"No," Dr. Hinken replied, "he's gotten to be quite the sailor. In fact, I'll feel safer with him along. An extra hand never hurts. No, just give him a change of clothes and a toothbrush. That's the great part about being a kid. Life's so simple. Well, if you have no other concerns, I'll let Dan and Kate know the good news. They're planning on leaving at nine sharp. We'll be looking for you at our place by eight, Pete. We're having a send-off breakfast so you sailors can rig the *Griffin* with a full stomach and be on your way in time to reach Mackinac by early afternoon."

At that, Dr. Hinken stood, shook hands with Pete's mom and dad, and headed back down the way to the *Polly Ann.*

"Well, Son," Howard Jenkins said, "it looks like you're in for a real, first-class sailing trip. Now, how about joining me in a few hours of hard labor repairing the dock."

CHAPTER 19
PREMONITION

10:00 p.m.

That night Pete lay in his bunk unable to sleep. The excitement of being with his friends and spying on the old man had been fun, but now that he'd had time to consider the consequences, he wondered if he wasn't getting himself mixed up in more than he could handle. What if the men he had heard in Mr. Geetings' cabin were real counterfeiters? It would be so easy for them to snuff out the lives of four kids who had stumbled onto the secret of their operation.

He finally dozed off only to awaken in a hot sweat from a nightmare that was so real that he could still see the headlines in the *Weekly Wave*:

> *Four Les Cheneaux Youths Missing.*
> *Sailboat Found Overturned In Straits.*
> *Three Boys, One Girl Blown To Bits."*

In the dream Harold Geetings was with someone in the black-hulled speedboat chasing the *Grif-*

fin in the middle of the Straits. He was blowing holes in the sailboat with a Gatling gun from about ten yards away while Pete and his friends held on for dear life from the top of the mast. It couldn't be a dream. It was more like a premonition. He lay there awake, unable to close his eyes.

A moment later, Pete's mom was nudging his shoulder. "Rise and shine, Pete," she said. "It's time for you to be going down to the Hinken's."

Pete jumped up, put on his new clothes, and went to the kitchen where he found his parents sitting at the table having coffee.

"Good morning, Morning Glory," his dad greeted him in his usual fashion.

"Are you okay?" his mom asked. "You look like you didn't sleep a wink."

"No, I'm fine," Pete said grabbing his toothbrush and pushing open the back porch screen door. "I just had a really strange dream, that's all." He brushed his teeth and scrubbed his face in a pan of cold water he had dipped from the catch tank. "Well, I'd better be going," he said shaking his toothbrush and stuffing it in his hip pocket.

He picked up his small overnight bag and, as he passed his bedroom, stepped in and gave his sister's bed a good shaking, "Bye, Cara," he whispered loudly. "Try to get along without me."

In moments he was past the Elliot Hotel onto Cincinnati Row. Pete hadn't even rounded the last bend in the path to Hinken's place when he heard Dan call out, "Hey, everybody, Pete's here."

Pete was beginning to sense that Dan had a talent for discerning the undiscernible. It was Dan who had asked him to join in the softball game without even knowing if he could play. It was Dan who tried to warn him when the *Griffin's* boom

96

nearly took his head off. It was Dan who had solved the envelope mystery and insisted they get off the old man's island when they did. Maybe Dan was simply more observant than Pete, but Pete was learning to trust Dan's intuitions. He wasn't just a friendly, fresh-faced, kid. He had a gift, either of clairvoyance or uncommon insight. And, for that matter, so had Kate. They always seemed to know what the other was thinking and doing.

Pete came into the clearing by the Hinken's front door. "I heard that, Dan," Pete laughed. "How'd you know I was here?"

"I've got great ears," Dan smiled. "I heard your front door close and I simply counted down. Come on in, you're just in time. We're having scrambled eggs, bacon, sausage, rolls, and strawberries. And that's just for starters."

"No, really," Pete pressed, "you seem to know what's going to happen before it actually does."

"Yes, well, I've noticed that you arrive at places just as food is being served," Dan replied. "I guess we all have our special talents, don't we?"

Come to think of it, Pete admitted, *I've never been accused of tardiness at mealtime. Still,* he thought, *it might not be a bad idea if they ever got in a tight spot to agree with one of Dan's hunches.*

Pete followed Dan into the Hinken's cottage. It was as festive a gathering as he had ever seen with tables of food and lots of people. He recognized everyone—not by name, certainly, but by their presence at all the social events Pete had attended. Ann Hinken offered him an empty plate and Butzie Terkel, Eddie's mom, encouraged him to fill it up.

"It's the last meal you'll get before Mackinac," she said. "Eddie won't be serving anything like this aboard the *Griffin.*"

Pete wolfed down as much as he could and then Butzie wrapped some sticky buns and stuffed them in his gym bag. Kate grabbed his arm and guided him to the boathouse. The foursome wouldn't have to deal with *A Little Dinghy* this day. Bill Terkel backed the *Silver Moon* out of her slip and met the sailors at the end of the dock. He escorted them to the *Griffin* and, in half an hour, she was rigged and ready.

"Cast off, lubber," Eddie called out to his father who laughed as he unhooked the bow line from the mooring ball and tossed it to Dan.

"Arrgh," Dan squinted as he hailed the crowd on the dock, "we're off for adventure on the high Northern seas, so we are, or me name's not Dangerous Dan, and that be the truth of the matter, heh heh."

As soon as Pete set the main sail, a sharp breeze filled her and the *Griffin* shot towards Elliot Bay. Eddie headed her past Mr. Geetings' island toward Reif's Point. Into Muscallonge Bay and out through Middle Entrance blew the *Griffin*. From there, Eddie drew a compass reading south of Goose Island and headed straight for Mackinac.

Dan struck up his favorite sea chantey in his best pirate-like, gravelly voice,

> *In South Australia I was born,*
> *Heave away, haul away,*
> *In South Australia, round Cape Horn,*
> *We're bound for South Australia . . .*

By ten o'clock, Kate was sunning herself on the starboard bow, while Dan was manning the tiller. Eddie was studying the Straits chart, and Pete went below for a nap. The *Griffin* was off Goose Island.

By one o'clock, Kate was rolling up the map, Dan was sunning himself on the starboard bow, Eddie was manning the tiller, and Pete was still asleep below. The *Griffin* was within sight of Mackinac.

By two o'clock, the *Griffin* was inside the two long breakwalls that protect Mackinac Island harbor from southeast winds. Kate was manning the tiller. Eddie was adjusting the jib, and Dan was checking out the yacht dock. Pete was coming up from below having missed everything but his appetite.

"Anyone want a roll?" he asked, blinking his eyes.

"Please?" Eddie replied.

Pete paused a moment, remembering the odd, Cincinnati expression. "Do you want a sticky bun?" he said louder.

"No," Eddie laughed. "I meant, `Yes, I'm starved.'"

"What else do you have stowed in there?" Dan asked.

"Sausages, blintzes, scrambled eggs—you name it," Pete said poking around the small satchel. "Eddie's mom must've thought we were sailing to Chicago, or something. How 'bout some hard-boiled eggs? I guess they're hard-boiled."

"Oh, Pete," Kate sounded relieved. "You were below deck so long, I was afraid you were seasick or something."

"No, I'm fine, Kate," Pete replied. "I just didn't sleep at all last night. I had the worst dream. Mr. Geetings was chasing us in his speedboat and blasting us in the *Griffin* from point blank. It was so real it was scary."

"Well, I think we should avoid the yacht dock," Dan suggested surveying the boats. "Let's slip around it and beach the *Griffin* out of sight on the other side of the coal dock. If Fats and Mr. Geetings are in cahoots, I'd just as soon they didn't know we were even here."

"Okay," Eddie said. "Kate, raise the center board and we'll beach her in front of the Lakeview. Drop the jib, Pete."

The *Griffin* was almost ashore when Pete had secured the jib. He looked up to see the village of Mackinac Island. It was spectacular. Each building sparkled, freshly painted, in the sun. Black and maroon horse-drawn carriages moved slowly along the narrow streets. Baskets of red flowers hung from every lamp post. People were peddling bicycles and walking along the avenues. There was an astonishing absence of cars, trucks, buses, gas stations, and, most of all, noise. The only sounds were those of the waves lapping softly on the shore and the distant clomping of horses' hooves weaving through the village streets. Even more remarkable was the peculiar mixture of the fresh scent of lilacs, the sweet aroma of fudge, and the pungent odor of horse urine wafting into the harbor.

"Hold on, Pete, we're coming ashore," Kate called out.

"Drop the main, Dan," Eddie ordered. "We'll coast in from here. Take the bow line, Pete. Jump ashore and pull us in."

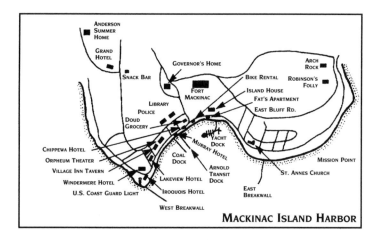

CHAPTER 20
MACKINAC ISLAND

Sunday, June 29 3:00 p.m.

They stowed the sails and drew the *Griffin* up onto the beach. Eddie locked the cabin door and pocketed the key.

"Well, fellow sleuths, now what?" Dan asked.

"I say we nose around the yacht dock," Eddie said.

"We've got to check in with Aunt Nancy," Kate insisted. "She'll call out the Coast Guard if she doesn't hear from us soon. Besides, I'm hungry."

"All right," Eddie resigned. "How about a race up to your aunt and uncle's. Pete and Dan against Kate and me."

"Okay, Eddie," Kate agreed. "How about it, Dan?"

"Fine with me. We'll start from the Orpheum Theater."

Dan motioned for Pete to stay close by his side. When the four reached the Village Inn Tavern, Dan grabbed Pete's arm and, with a sly grin, pulled him back. The two raced around a corner and up a narrow side street.

101

"We'll hop on the back of a cab going up to the Grand," Dan said as soon as Eddie and Kate were out of sight.

The two boys hurried up the hill where, as they neared Market Street, a tall, black carriage drawn by two horses approached from behind. The driver was wearing a maroon uniform and a cap marked, "Taxi," in gold letters.

"I can't believe our luck," Dan whispered to his partner. "This is perfect. Keep walking like nothing's happening. When I say `go,' follow me. Once he's past us, we'll cut behind him and hop on the back luggage rack. Two people can get away with it, but if three try, the driver can tell something's wrong. He calls out `Whoa' to his team and grabs the stowaways. He binds and gags them and publicly throws them off the end of the Arnold Transit dock."

"Oh, okay. So it's pretty safe then, eh?" Pete mumbled. "But you better be kidding about that last part."

"Ri-i-ight now!" Dan whispered as he stepped off the sidewalk. They took three, long strides and eased themselves onto the back ledge as it rolled along. Dan smiled, "See? Easy."

Pete just shook his head. "I'm on Mackinac Island five minutes and already I'm risking being thrown off."

As they bounced along Market Street, Dan peeked around to the front. "Stay put, Pete. I'll be right back." Dan slipped off and darted down the street.

"Where are you going?" Pete whispered frantically.

Dan turned his head and put a finger to his lips. He hurried up to a small newspaper rack on the sidewalk. A woman was just inserting the latest edition of the local paper as Dan approached. He grabbed an issue and raced back to the carriage.

"It's the *Mackinac Island Town Crier*," Dan said with mock enthusiasm. "It's got all the latest gossip."

The carriage continued along the wide, maple tree-lined boulevard as Dan poured over the small newspaper. "Look at this!" Dan said holding the paper just out of Pete's line of vision. *"Four Les Cheneaux Youths Missing: Sailboat Found Drifting In Straits. Bullet Holes Riddle Ship and Crew.'"*

Pete jerked his head toward the newspaper. "Where?"

"Made you look!" Dan snickered.

"Cut that out," Pete laughed nervously.

Dan turned the page. "Well, I'll be," he said. "There goes our mystery. Listen to this. *'Local Author Introduces Novel—Book Signing Monday, June 30 At Grand Hotel.'* Seriously, Pete, it's Mr. Geetings in the picture standing in the middle of a bunch of men."

"Are you sure? Let me see that." Pete leaned over and glanced at the photo as the carriage bumped along the road past a stone church. "It's him, all right," Pete said, sitting back. "For once, I'm glad my sister was right. I guess Mr. Geetings really was carrying books out to his island all along. I can't believe we wasted so much time spying on him."

"I don't understand how I could have been so wrong," Dan replied absently. "I just wonder. Some things still don't add up."

"Well, it's a load off my mind," Pete said, relaxing against a leather suitcase. "You worry about the math. I'm going to explore the island instead."

Dan shook his head, looked around, and noticed that the carriage was approaching the Grand Hotel. "Time to bid our fellow passengers adieu, Pete. Here's our stop."

He folded the *Town Crier* and jammed it into his duffle bag. They slipped off the luggage rack and ambled toward the front of the landmark hotel. Dan stopped at the corner by a small door marked, "Employees Only." As Pete caught up to him, Dan glanced quickly in all directions, grabbed Pete by the arm, and pulled him through the entrance.

Inside the hotel, they walked briskly through the employees' dining area. Pete hadn't noticed the warning on the door, so he sauntered along the aisle a few steps behind Dan checking out the wall-length mural.

"This is really something," Pete said.

"Well, we're not exactly supposed to be here," Dan whispered, "so kindly keep your art critiques to yourself."

"Not again," Pete mumbled. "How many places on this island are off limits?"

"You've got to learn your way around, Pete. Besides, you don't want Kate and Eddie to beat us, do you?"

They came to the carriage landing at the hotel's front entrance. Pete followed as Dan raced up the bellboys' service stairway. He opened a small, white door and led Pete smack into the spacious hotel lobby. Pete could barely walk through the inch-thick carpet.

"Can I relax now?" Pete asked.

"Well, I suppose you could," Dan smiled, "if you were wearing a jacket and tie."

Pete shot a look in each direction. Everyone, even the little kids, were dressed up like church. Pete just shook his head.

They dashed through another door and down a long hallway. Daylight at the end grew brighter as the two hurried past tall doors with silver-plated numbers.

Passing the last guest room, they brushed through a swinging gate which Pete read, as it closed behind him, "Private—Hotel Guests Only." He stepped off the end of the world's longest porch into the cool, fresh, Straits of Mackinac air.

Pete glanced out over the open water and saw what appeared to be a miniature ferryboat. He looked closer. It was the *Munising*, the largest of the fleet. Pete followed Dan as they walked along a carriage path.

"See? We made it," Dan smiled. "Nothing to worry about. Aunt Nancy and Uncle George's cottage is just ahead."

Pete looked to his right. The West Bluff homes that had resembled small cabins next to the Grand Hotel from across the water, now looked like hotels, themselves.

As they walked along the path, a black, one-horse hansom clomped past them and stopped in front of the fifth house. Pete could see that this was the most extraordinary of all the incredible mansions. Its towers and balconies and turrets overlooked the west bluff from its highest point and a flag waved majestically in the Straits breeze. He became anxious to think he might actually see someone who lived in such a magnificent residence. Out stepped an elegantly dressed lady assisted by a coachman. She was followed immediately by two younger people. It was Kate and Eddie.

"Ha, we beat you," they said pointing at Dan and Pete. The woman, Pete realized, was Mrs. Anderson, or Aunt Nancy to Dan and Kate. And this was her cottage.

"Welcome, everyone," she smiled and placed her hands on Pete's shoulders. "Now, you must be Pete Jenkins. I've heard so much about you." She stepped back and spoke to all of her guests. "You're probably exhausted from your sail, so Charles, here," she motioned to the carriage driver, "will show you to your rooms. You may put your belongings away and freshen up. We'll meet in the drawing room for a light snack in, say, half an hour."

In all his fifteen years, Pete had never been given an expressed opportunity to "freshen up." The four guests followed Charles to the second floor where each was ushered into his own room overlooking the bluff.

Pete opened the door and stood gaping into his gymnasium-sized bedroom, his small suitcase clutched in his left hand. Two spacious windows were open, a breath of Straits air gently swirling the lace curtains. He stepped inside closing the tall, wooden door behind him. He was still blinking, taking in the enormous size of his room, when an anxious knock sounded behind him.

"Pete. Are you in there?" It was Dan.

"Uh huh," Pete replied absently.

Dan rushed in holding the *Town Crier*. He was followed by Eddie and Kate.

"Take a look at this," Dan said opening the paper to the back page.

The Anderson's Summer Home

CHAPTER 21
THE MYSTERY

5:00 p.m.

Pete sat down in a white wicker rocking chair near the window and began to read.

Book Signing: continued from Page 2.

Mr. Harold Geetings will be accompanied by the book's publisher, Mr. James Barnwell, who describes *Mackinac Passage* as a sure-fire literary success for his Los Angeles publishing house. Movie rights have already been sold to a major motion picture studio. Filming will begin here next summer.

"Los Angeles?" Pete said. "Weren't the boxes you helped Mr. Geetings put on his boat postmarked from New York?"

"That's right, Pete," Kate replied. "But that's not all. Look at this." She pointed to another headline:

Counterfeit Bills Reported By Local Hotel.

Mr. Ronald Dufina, day manager at the Murray Hotel, reported to local police that receipts from the previous night's dinner revenue revealed five $20's with identical serial numbers. Bartender, Jeff Frazier and waitress, Danna Wolke, both Michigan State College students and summer employees of the Murray Hotel, feel certain they could identify the person who passed the bogus bills.

Island business owners and staff are cautioned to be on the alert for the replicas bearing the serial number B66867611I.

"Well," Pete sighed sitting back in his chair. "It looks like we're back in the mystery business."

It was clear that Mr. Geetings had written a book. But it had been published in California. Whatever was being sent to him from New York wasn't his novel. Pete stood up. "Wait a minute. Let me see that picture again!" He flipped the newspaper back to the second page. "The man in the picture with Mr. Geetings, that's Mr. Barnwell. I'd forgotten his name but he's the one who bought my muskie and paid me with two fake twenties."

"So, he's mixed up in this, too!" Kate said.

Pete thought for a moment. "No, I don't think so. He said right away that he was going to call the police. He must have done it because I saw him turn the fake money over to two state troopers on the porch of the Elliot Hotel that night."

"Okay," Dan said, "but that doesn't change what

we saw and heard on the old man's island. I still think Geetings is involved."

"I don't understand," Eddie said. "If the old man wrote such a famous book, he must have made a lot of money for it. Why would he risk being part of an illegal money scheme?"

"Who knows?" Kate replied. "But Dan's right. He's tangled up in it somehow."

"I think we should go to your aunt and uncle and tell them what we know right now," Eddie said.

"Not yet," Kate disagreed. "Not until we can prove it. Aunt Nancy and Uncle George will think we're here just looking for mischief. Besides, they'll be sure to tell our parents and that will be the end of our trips to Mackinac."

"How about if we go to the police," Pete said.

"That won't work, either," Dan replied. "There's only one policeman on this island and he's good friends with my uncle. If we don't show him positive proof, he'll call Uncle George. That would be worse than us telling him ourselves."

The four spent the next fifteen minutes in Pete's room discussing the options.

———

"Okay," Eddie said. "We'll start by going to the yacht dock to see if Mr. Geetings' speedboat is there."

"Right," Dan agreed. "Let's head downstairs and tell Aunt Nancy we're going to show Pete around town."

"It's almost 5:30," Kate noticed. "We'd better hurry."

"If we're late," Pete smiled, "you can blame it on me. I hardly ever freshen up in anything under an hour."

They tore down the wide, circular stairway and found Mr. and Mrs. Anderson seated around a coffee table filled with cheese and crackers. George Anderson was dressed in a blue blazer and white slacks. He was tall, dark, and very dignified. He wore a warm, welcoming smile and a red, polka dot bow tie. Nancy Anderson, likewise, was smashing.

"I know you're all hungry," Mr. Anderson said, "but don't fill up on snacks. We'll be sitting down for dinner right at seven."

"Now, for the wonderful news," Nancy Anderson announced. "Harold Geetings, a dear friend of ours, will be joining us for lunch tomorrow. He's recently published a novel that is set in the Straits. Tomorrow at noon he'll be holding a press conference from our veranda."

"Even though he lives in the Snows," George Anderson added, "you probably don't know him. He guards his privacy like a recluse. I assure you, however, that you will remember this occasion for as long as you live."

The four guests' alarmed expressions could not have been more misinterpreted.

"Well," Mr. Anderson continued, looking from one somber face to another, "I can understand why people your age might not be interested in literary affairs, but I promise you, when you meet Mr. Geetings, you will find him to be a most fascinating gentleman. His novel will be the topic of many of this summer's social conversations."

The four friends looked at one another in disbelief. The very man they had pursued for the past three weeks and proven to themselves at least, to be a criminal, turned out to be their hosts' most esteemed acquaintance and guest of honor for one of this summer's highlights.

"Oh, we're excited, all right," Dan mumbled. "Actually, we know quite a lot about Mr. Geetings, but, as you say, none of us have ever met him. Except maybe for Pete. Isn't that right, Pete."

"Uh, that's right, um, pretty much. My mom knew him years ago, and I've bumped into him, I mean, you know, seen him a lot, but I doubt if he knows me. We've never actually been introduced. He likes to be by himself, I guess. Writers are like that, my mom says."

"Well, Aunt Nancy, Uncle George," Dan said as he arose from his chair, "we thought we'd go into town for a while. Show Pete around."

"All right," Mr. Anderson said, "but don't ruin your appetites on fudge. Would you like Charles to take you in the carriage?"

"Oh, no, thanks," Dan replied. "But if you still have the bikes in the barn, it would be faster if we could use them."

"Certainly," Mr. Anderson said. "They're all oiled and ready to go."

"That's great," Kate spoke up. She turned to her friends. "Let's make tracks, guys."

Pete followed Kate out the back door. They found several well-polished bicycles stored in the spacious carriage barn behind the house. Each chose one, hopped on, and pedalled along the service path behind the west bluff homes. From there Dan led them along the road behind the Grand Hotel golf course and down the steep trail by the fort into town. Stopping beside Doud's Grocery Store in front of the Coast Guard station, they looked over at the yacht dock hoping to see the mystery speedboat. Or Mr. Geetings. Or Fats.

"Do you think Fats will remember us from our last trip?" Kate asked.

"I don't know," Eddie replied, "but I'll bet Mr. Geetings recognizes us from the day we helped him with the boxes. Anyway, the longer we can avoid them, the better off we'll be."

"Well," Dan said, "if the speedboat is still tied up in its old well, we won't be able to see it unless we walk right out to the end of the dock."

"Okay, let's go," Kate agreed. They got back on their bikes and pedaled slowly toward the marina.

CHAPTER 22
FATS

6:00 p.m.

They leaned their two-wheelers against a cannon near the shore and walked toward the head of the yacht dock. As they passed the bike rental, a pale, thin man was running a chain through the frames of a long line of bicycles, locking them for the day. When he glanced up at the four youths, Pete, who was the closest to him, couldn't help noticing how out of place he appeared. He wore a dark, shiny suit with a gray, silk shirt open at the neck. His long black hair was slicked back and his shoes were thin and pointed. Pete knew this guy didn't fit in the picture, but he didn't know why. The man curled his lip at Pete.

Pete turned and hurried to catch up with his friends as they walked along the waterfront. Eddie led the way past a small, white building with two signs. The first sign read, "Dockmaster's Quar-

ters," and the second, "Marina Comfort Station—
Restrooms & Showers, Members Only."

They walked about a hundred feet out onto the
wide, wood-planked dock when Eddie stopped.
"There she is," he whispered pointing to the fur-
thest boat on the east side. Although a tarp covered it from stem to stern, it was, unquestionably,
the mystery boat. Its hull was so low in the water
that the finger pier was a foot above the boat's deck.
Eddie went alongside, kneeled down and lifted the
tarp.

"Hey!" a man shouted from a few feet behind.

The four spun around to see a tall, thin man
wearing a dark, shiny suit with a grey, silk shirt
open at the neck.

"Get away from dat boat, see? What youse doin'
hangin' 'roun' 'ere?"

Eddie hopped to his feet. "We just stopped to
look at this speedboat. Is it yours?"

"None o' your biz. G'wan, git otta here. Beat
it!"

Pete recognized him immediately but was too
surprised to speak. The four walked quickly to the
farthest slip on the other end of the yacht dock.

Pete glanced back to see if the man was still
watching them. Seeing that he wasn't, he whispered, "That's the guy we just passed along the
shore who was closing up the bike rental."

"You're kidding?" Eddie said. "Who is he to care
if we're on the dock?"

"I don't know," Danny replied, "but he certainly
got excited when you lifted that tarp."

"You're right, Dan," Kate agreed. "I'll just bet
he's mixed up in this counterfeit scheme, too. Why
else would he be so anxious about some kids looking at boats?"

114

"Did anyone see where he went?" Eddie asked.

"He walked back down the dock," Pete answered, "and into that little white building."

"That's where Fats lives!" Kate said.

"You know what?" Dan said, "I got a hunch it was Fats and that guy right there that we heard arguing on Mr. Geetings' island. I say we hang around here for awhile and see if anything happens?"

"I'm with you," Kate said, "but we'd better stay out of sight. I've got an idea. I'll slip into the comfort station. The last time I was here I used that bathroom and heard two men's voices so clearly, I was afraid to move."

"An air duct probably connects the bathrooms to Fats' apartment," Eddie said.

"Now that I think of it," Kate added, "one of those voices that day sounded like that skinny guy who shooed us off the dock just now. He had that same funny accent."

They hadn't taken five steps along the dock when out of the dockmaster's building came the thin man. He walked down the steps and turned toward town.

"Now's our chance." Eddie said. "Dan, follow that guy. Pete, stay with me. Kate, you go into the comfort station and listen for any conversation you can hear."

In moments, all four were in place. Five minutes passed. Eddie and Pete waited behind a large lilac bush twenty feet from the door.

"Look," Pete whispered pointing up the street.

"It's Geetings," Eddie said, "and he's coming our way. Stay out of sight."

Harold Geetings was carrying a thin newspaper under his arm. He stopped in front of Fats' apartment, looked in all directions, and then slipped through the door.

Soon, Pete and Eddie heard muffled voices from inside.

"I'd like to make sure that it's Fats who's in there with Mr. Geetings," Eddie whispered to Pete. "I hope Kate can hear what they're saying."

"We can't wait much longer," Pete said. "We have to get back. Mr. Anderson told us not to be late for dinner."

"You're right. I've got an idea," Eddie said. "Listen, Pete. Go to the end of the dock and then turn around. Walk like you're just out for a stroll, but watch Fats' front door. Keep on coming until you get past the dockmaster's quarters. Then follow the shoreline into town. Got it?"

"I've got it," Pete said, looking confused, "but I don't get it."

"You will," Eddie said. "There's no time to explain."

Pete went out to the end of the dock, turned and began toward shore. He could see Eddie watching him from behind the lilac bush. Then Eddie sprang from his hiding place and charged up to Fats' room. He hammered the door hard, three times with his fist. Pete almost fainted as Eddie ran around the building, crossed the road, and hurried up a path alongside the Island House Hotel. Suddenly the dockmaster's door flew open and an enormous man burst through it.

Fats glanced in all directions, fire practically shooting from his eyes. He stared at the teenage boy casually ambling toward him. He dismissed him as an unlikely suspect and raced around to the other side of the building.

Eddie had run to the front of the Island House Hotel and stretched himself out on a lawn chair pretending to be asleep. He kept one eye on Fats and the other on the waterfront where Pete was walking, somewhat unsteadily, into town. He drew a sigh of relief when Pete disappeared around the Coast Guard station. Then he realized that Fats had begun to move toward the comfort station doors. He wouldn't dare walk into the women's bathroom, would he?

Fats used his master key to open the men's room door and stepped inside. The moment the door sprang shut, Kate slipped out of the women's room letting the latch close silently. She dashed around the corner and hurried along the shore into town.

Eddie sneaked across the front lawns of the summer homes from the Island House to Father Marquette Park. From there he could see his three friends converging near the Chippewa Hotel. They met on the sidewalk, each with a story to tell and no time to tell it.

"You won't believe what I just saw!" Dan said.

"You won't believe what I just did," Eddie followed.

"I can't believe any of this," Pete muttered. "If we don't watch ourselves, we're going to end up in a peck of trouble."

"I think we already have," Kate agreed. "Let's get back to Aunt and Uncle's."

CHAPTER 23
FOUR TALES

6:50 p.m.

They sneaked back to the cannon, grabbed their bikes, and raced toward the west bluff. About half-way up the hill to the Grand, Pete began to struggle. He couldn't pedal any further as he approached the Snack Bar, but neither could Eddie, Dan, or Kate. Eddie and Dan hopped off their bikes anxious to tell their part of what had just happened in town.

Dan started, even before he'd slid off his seat. "I followed that skinny guy after he left the yacht dock. First, he went into Alford's Drug Store and bought a tin of aspirin. He gave the clerk a crisp twenty dollar bill. She gave him change, and he was out the door. Then, just as I approached the cash register, she started after him. When she saw me, though, she stopped and said, `Well, I guess if he has a headache, he'll be back. He left his aspirin. What can I help you with?' I told her that I needed a new twenty dollar bill for my cousin's birthday party. I held out two fives and a ten. She said she'd just gotten this one from the guy with the aspirin.

"Now, check out the serial number," Dan said as he held the counterfeit twenty up for the others to see.

"It can't be fake," Pete said. "Look at those red and blue threads in the paper. Even the best counterfeits don't have those. My sister said so."

Dan pulled the *Town Crier* article from his hip pocket. "Here, Pete. Look for yourself, B668676611I."

"That's the number, all right, threads or no threads."

"Now we've got some real evidence," Dan concluded.

"Then what happened?" Eddie asked.

"Well, I ran out the door. I thought he'd gotten away in the crowd but I caught a glimpse of him going into the Pink Pony Tavern at the Chippewa Hotel. I hurried into the lobby. He ordered a beer and paid the bartender with another new twenty. He didn't seem to be in such a rush this time, so I decided I'd better find you. He's in with Fats and Geetings, no question about that. What did you three find out?"

Eddie and Pete told how they had seen Mr. Geetings go into Fats' room and what Eddie had done to make Fats show himself.

"It was Fats, all right," Pete assured everyone. "I've never been so scared in all my life. He blasted out of that door and just about stared a hole right through me."

"Hey, Kate, were you able to hear anything from the bathroom?" Eddie asked.

Kate had been walking along pushing her bike quietly. "I heard plenty but I don't want to talk about it," Kate said. Eddie and Dan looked at each other. This was unprecedented. Kate knew something important that she didn't want to share.

Dan ran ahead taking hold of her handlebars. "What do you mean?" he whispered.

"Listen, Dan," Kate began grimly. "There isn't any other way out of this. We've just got to make Aunt and Uncle believe us. They're the only ones who can help."

"Come on, Kate," Eddie reminded her. "With that fake twenty that Dan got, they can't help but believe us. Besides, if you'd rather not tell them first, we could go right to the police chief. That should be plenty of evidence to get his attention."

"No, we can't," Kate replied. "Not with what I just heard. Okay, here's what happened. I waited under that ventilating duct for several minutes, then a door opened. After it closed, someone said, `Look what Cahill's done now!' Then I heard papers shuffling."

"That must have been Geetings," Eddie interrupted. He went into Fats' place with the *Town Crier.*"

"Well, there was silence for a moment," Kate continued. "Then I heard another voice, Fats, I guess, let out a string of horrible obscenities. Then he said he'd have to make sure that Cahill didn't blow the whole deal. Then Geetings said, `We've got to get him off the island,' and Fats says, `We'll have to do better than that. And we'll have to do it tonight.'

120

"'What do you mean by that?' Geetings said. And Fats says, 'You know what I mean. If all we do is send him packing, he'll be back next week with the mob and we'll be fish food. It's him or us, old man.'

"Then Mr. Geetings asked where Joey was. Fats said he had gone into town to get a beer. 'What are we going to do about those two college kids that saw him at the Lamplighter?' Mr. Geetings asked. 'Don't worry about them,' Fats said. 'Jack Chamberlain is the only cop in town, and we've got him paid off. He'll cover our tracks there.'

"Now," Kate concluded, "don't you see? We've got to convince Aunt Nancy and Uncle George to help us."

"Who's Cahill?" Pete asked.

"He must be the skinny guy I followed into town," Dan replied. "Joey Cahill."

"It's got to be," Eddie added. "And Dan's right. It had to have been Fats and Joey Cahill arguing that day on the old man's island."

"We'd better get back for dinner," Dan said.

They hopped on their bikes and raced behind the Grand Hotel to the Anderson's horse barn. Putting the two-wheelers inside, they ran across the path and up the back steps of the summer home.

"Oh, here you are," Nancy Anderson greeted the four. "You're right on time. Run upstairs and get ready for dinner."

121

Carriage Barn

CHAPTER 24
DINNER

7:15 p.m.

Zachary, the chef, pushed open the swinging, kitchen door carrying a monstrous, silver platter of beef tenderloin. Pete's first three hours on the island, as eventful as they had been, were momentarily forgotten.

"I understand, Peter, that you've never been to Mackinac," Mrs. Anderson said from one end of the long, dining room table.

"That's right, ma'am," Pete replied. "It's a very exciting place."

"Interesting observation, Peter," Mrs. Anderson said. "We'd rather think of it as restful and relaxing, but I suppose to someone who's not been here, it may seem exciting."

"Then this is a special occasion," Mr. Anderson directed to Pete. "I'd like to propose a toast." He lifted his glass and said, "May your visit be restful, exciting, and memorable."

As the four friends raised their glasses, each glanced at one another. They knew it would be memorable and exciting, all right. It was already that. But without the Anderson's help, their stay might be entirely too restful, in a permanent sort of way. Someone would have to explain to the Andersons what had happened in town. Pete was glad the other three were good talkers because, he was sure, it wasn't going to be him.

When everyone was finished with the main course, Charles whisked the plates from the table and Zachary reappeared with *Peach Flambe*. Other than overdoing a marshmallow, Pete had never seen anybody deliberately set fire to a perfectly good dessert. It looked like some sort of ritual sacrifice to the Goddess of Opulence.

When Zachary returned to the kitchen, Mrs. Anderson said, "We're so thrilled about our luncheon tomorrow with Harold Geetings. His novel is set here in the Straits, you know."

George Anderson added, "Mrs. Anderson and I have known the Geetings family since we were children. Harold took such a long, lonely path in life, writing for months on end with nothing to show for it. His family fortune dwindled but he always stayed in touch and visited us when he could. Now he's finally become a published author. We're so proud of him and so happy to have been even a small part of his success."

"I'm moved to tears," Mrs. Anderson continued, "when I think how diligently he's worked, the deprivation he's endured, and the heartache he's suffered living such a solitary life for his art."

The four glanced again at each other. Eventually, all eyes fell on Dan. He waited a moment, cleared his throat, and began. "Speaking of Mr. Geetings," he said, "we saw him down at the yacht dock this afternoon. We think we have something very important to tell you."

"Oh, how wonderful," Mrs. Anderson beamed. "While you were there, did you happen to meet Mr. FitzRoberts, the dockmaster? He's such a jolly man, a true ambassador for Mackinac Island. And he's so helpful in our community, too. Whenever Mr. Chamberlain, our policeman, needs help, Fats, as he seems to prefer, is always there to help. But, I'm sorry, Dan. What were you saying? You spoke with Mr. Geetings at the yacht dock?"

"Well," Dan hesitated. "No, uh, we didn't really speak to him so much as we saw him under some odd circumstances."

"Uncle George," Kate interrupted, "have you heard about the counterfeit money that was being passed in town?"

"Yes, Kate," Mr. Anderson responded. "I read the article in today's *Town Crier*. I went right down to Jack Chamberlain, the police chief. He showed me the currency that had been turned over by Mr. Dufina, the manager of the Murray Hotel. They weren't counterfeit at all, just brand new bills with consecutive numbers. Chief Chamberlain also said that those two college students working at the Lamplighter couldn't even agree if the person they had seen was a man or a woman. I'm afraid the reporters at the *Town Crier* are just too irresponsible for such an important assignment."

"Well, Uncle George," Dan said reaching into his pocket, "I'd like to show you this." He passed the twenty dollar bill to Mr. Anderson. "I got this in town an hour ago from someone we're sure is linked to the counterfeit scheme. It has the same serial number as the one reported in the newspaper. It must be a fake."

Mr. Anderson looked carefully at the twenty. "Well, I'll be. I can only guess that Chief Chamberlain released the five bills back into circulation as he said he would. You must have just been in the right place at the right time. Quite a coincidence, I'd say. But Jack couldn't be mistaken. He's been serving this island for thirty years. I would trust him with my life. However, if you think there might be a question about this currency, I'm sure he'd like to know about it. Why don't you go into town and talk to him right now. I'll call him myself and arrange for a meeting."

"No, that's okay," Eddie jumped in. He knew that getting the crooked policeman involved would be the worst thing they could do. Also, he knew Mr. Anderson didn't really believe Dan. "I'm sure the bill that Dan got was just a coincidence like you said. Right, Dan?"

"Yes, it must be," Dan replied. "And we sure wouldn't want to bother Mr. Chamberlain. Thanks, Uncle George. I suppose we just got carried away with the excitement of the counterfeit money mystery."

So much for the straight forward approach, Pete thought at once. *But now, what?*

Now what, indeed.

Mackinac Harbor

CHAPTER 25
THE PLAN

9:00 p.m.

Mr. Anderson looked at his watch and slid his chair back from the dining room table. Although the sun was still fairly high in the northwest sky, it was close to nine o'clock.

"Well, sailors, it's time for me to call your parents. Is there anything you want me to tell them?" George Anderson asked as he dialed the Cedarville exchange. He glanced at each anxious face, but no one replied.

"Hello, Dan. This is George. . . . No, everything's fine. Well, they seem a bit tired from the sail. They'll probably turn in early. . . . Yes. It's too bad you can't be here tomorrow. We're holding a press conference for Harold Geetings' new book. . . . Sure, I'll get you a signed copy. Okay, I'll call you in the morning . . . Give Ann my love. . . . Uh huh, . . . Bye, Dan."

"You kids probably want to get to bed early," Nancy Anderson said, getting up from the table, "after your long sail and all. But, you're welcome to stay up and watch us play bridge with the Sweeneys. They're due any minute."

"Well," Kate said looking out the bay window, "it looks like we've got about another hour of daylight. Maybe we'll ride back into town. We met some people this afternoon who invited us to a party at the yacht dock."

Kate had hatched up a plan over dessert. The more she thought about it, the more it seemed like a brilliant ploy.

"Let's go, guys."

Eddie and Pete picked up on her interest wondering what she had dreamed up this time. Dan seemed to know.

"Right," Pete said, pushing his chair back. "Let's get while the gettin's good," not really sure what the gettin' was that he was gettin' into.

"We'll be back before dark," Dan said to his aunt and uncle. "May we use the bikes again?"

"Charles keeps them polished just for you," George Anderson smiled.

"Thanks for the terrific meal, Mr. and Mrs. Anderson," Pete said. "You know, that's the first supper I've had in a month that someone didn't use a hook and line to catch."

"You're welcome, Pete," Mrs. Anderson laughed. "Bye, kids. Have fun in town. Don't be too late."

"All right, Kate," Eddie said, sliding open the heavy, carriage barn door. "What do you have up your sleeve?"

"Okay," Kate began. "Aunt and Uncle aren't against us. They're just don't believe us. Yet. All we need is one more piece of hard evidence. The more I thought about what Fats and Geetings said this afternoon, the more I realized we have to get to Joey Cahill tonight."

"Are you kidding?" Eddie exclaimed. "Cahill wouldn't listen to us! He'd grab us and take us to Fats."

"No, he wouldn't," Dan interrupted as though he and Kate had somehow pieced this plan together over bitefuls of *Peach Flambe*. "First, we'll show him the article in the *Town Crier*. Then Kate will tell him what she heard Fats say at the yacht dock. Unless he's a total nitwit, he's got to know we're his only chance."

"And he's our only chance," Kate added, checking her watch. "But we'll have to catch him before Fats and Mr. Geetings do. He might still be at the Pink Pony."

Eddie finally nodded and picked up his bike. "All right," he said, "but we'd better get to him where lots of people are around."

"Let's go," Kate urged. "There's no time to waste."

They flew down the hill into town and leaned their bicycles against the side of Doud's Grocery. Before crossing the street to the Pink Pony, Dan glanced back toward the marina. He nudged the other three when he saw Fats and Mr. Geetings walking down the steps from Fats' apartment toward town. The four hurried across the street to the Chippewa Hotel just as Joey Cahill sauntered out of the Pink Pony. They were too late. They watched helplessly as he swaggered along the sidewalk toward the marina. Joey stopped at the rental booth to check the locks.

"Cahill!" Fats called out.

Joey turned. He stood and waited for Fats and Geetings to meet him. As they talked, Joey motioned toward the Pink Pony. Fats pointed the opposite way toward Mission Point.

"So much for plan `A'," Eddie whispered.

"It looks like Fats is getting his way," Dan added. "They're heading out of town."

"Let's follow them," Kate said. "Maybe they'll split up. If we can get to Joey for five minutes, we still might have a chance."

Although there was plenty of daylight, the shadows were lengthening and visibility was becoming difficult. The three men walked past Fats' apartment toward Mission Point. Fats talked and laughed, glancing warily in all directions.

"Okay," Eddie said, "we've gone this far. If we're going to follow them, we'd better do it right. We can't let them see us together. I'm the fastest runner. I'll stay just close enough to keep them in sight. Dan, you follow me. Kate, you follow Dan. Pete, keep your eye on Kate. We'll stay as far apart as we can. If they see one of us, we'll all scatter and meet back at the *Griffin*. Okay?"

Everyone nodded.

A block past Ste. Anne's Church, the three men turned left and started up the steep, winding embankment to the east bluff. They laughed and told jokes all the way up the hill. When they reached the top, they continued on the carriage path toward Arch Rock.

Eddie followed deep in the shadows.

Harold Geetings hesitated and looked back down the cliff to see if anyone was following them. In the distance, he saw a scruffy looking, tan-faced boy starting up the hill.

Pete dropped his eyes as soon as he saw Mr. Geetings staring at him. He tried to focus on the path ahead but his mind was fixed on the old man at the edge of the bluff. Pete quickly decided to make a diversionary move by turning onto a small, side street. He desperately wanted to spin on his heels and run, but he knew Mr. Geetings would strike out after him and run smack into his three friends along the way.

___

Harold Geetings stood for a moment, staring at the teenaged boy who walked nervously at the bottom of the hill. He knew him from somewhere. But where? When the boy went onto another path, Harold turned and rejoined Fats.

"What's keeping you, old man," Fats called back.

"Nothing, I guess," Harold replied, shaking his head.

The three men came to a small footpath marked *Robinson's Folly* and followed it into the woods. The trail led them through thirty yards of heavy brush and into a clearing a few feet from the edge of the cliff.

"I must be getting old," Fats said jokingly to Cahill. "I can't go anywhere without getting winded."

"Walkin' 'round wit' all o' dat blubber don't make it easy, right, Fat Boy?" Joey taunted.

"Yeah, heh, heh," Fats laughed through his clenched teeth. "We'll just rest here a minute," he said as he reached into his jacket pocket and pulled out a pint of Jim Beam. "How 'bout a pull while we talk over our plans?"

The three men sat with their arms resting on the bottom rung of the split-rail fence, their feet dangling over the edge of the two-hundred foot precipice. Mission Point lay in shadows below and Round Island Light flashed in the distance with the sun setting in the northwest.

―――

Eddie watched where the three men had left the trail. He followed and found a hiding place of birches and rocks about fifteen yards from where the three men sat. He looked back and motioned for Dan to approach, putting his index finger to his lips. Soon Kate and Pete also joined. The sun was sinking fast and it was becoming more difficult to see. Whatever the three men were discussing, it was much more serious than a few minutes before.

"Sun's been down for awhile," Eddie whispered nervously. "Soon, it'll be pitch dark. My guess is that nothing's going to happen. The old man must have talked some sense into Fats after we left them at the yacht dock. They're probably just planning their next move."

"Yeah," Pete agreed. "Let's get out of here. Maybe we can talk to Cahill tomorrow."

"Shh. Hold on," Dan cautioned. "Fats is doing something with his jacket."

The huge dockmaster came to his feet slowly extracting a short, club-like object from the sleeve of his coat. The old man remained seated, his head down. Joey Cahill rose to his feet, taking a step back from the railing but still looking out into the Straits.

Fats gripped the blackjack with both of his hands. He glanced to his right, looking at Cahill. He spun his massive body gaining momentum as he turned. He extended his arms and slammed the heavy club into the back of Joey Cahill's head.

An ominous crunch was the only sound the four heard. Joey Cahill's knees buckled as his lifeless body fell slowly forward onto the railing. He twitched slightly and slid down to the ground at Harold's side.

Fats sneered at his victim. "Call me `Fat Boy,' will you, you scrawny little punk."

He extended his right foot giving the inert body a nudge. It slid off the bluff and dropped eighty feet straight down before bouncing off a long, protruding boulder. It crashed through the underbrush and came to rest at the base of a jack pine. Cahill's corpse lay completely hidden both from the shore road below and the cliff above.

"Let's get out of here," Fats growled to the old man.

Harold Geetings sat staring out over Round Island.

"Look, Harold. It was his own fault. It was either him or us. Besides, now those two Murray Hotel kids can't link us. Let's go."

Harold Geetings slowly got to his feet and the two turned from the murder site. The old man trudged behind Fats who walked hurriedly back to the east bluff road. They strode directly toward the four terrified youths who were ducked deep into the rock and tree formation.

Pete felt the blood drain from his head when he realized what the club had done to Joey Cahill's brain. Fats and Geetings were almost alongside when he realized he was going to throw up. If he were at home in bed, he'd have just enough time to get to the bathroom. How he wished he were there right now with his mom saying what a brave little soldier he was and his dad holding his feverish forehead. He could only suppress it a few more moments. "Not now, please," he prayed.

One set of heavy footsteps passed within three feet of the four youths. Pete's eyes were closed; his head was spinning. Moments later, another set plodded slowly behind the first. Water was pouring from Pete's eyes and nose. His stomach was churning wildly. He couldn't hold it any more.

———

Thirty yards in the distance where the foot path meets the road, Fats stopped and wheeled around. "Harold! Did you hear that?"

"No," the old man said. But he had. And he knew it had something to do with the boy he'd seen on the walking path. Pete's face flashed through his mind again. He knew he'd seen him somewhere before. Somewhere recently. Not on Mackinac. In the Snows. Yes, he'd seen him in the Snows. He could almost picture him on a boat. Or by a screen door. Who was he?

Robinsons Folly

CHAPTER 26
FLIGHT

10:00 p.m.

"No, you deaf old fool," Fats yelled into Harold Geetings' ear as he charged back along the path. "I heard someone barfing his guts out. Whoever it was, saw what happened to Cahill. We've got to get him now."

The old man followed Fats back into the grove. Pete regained control of himself and the four clung to each other crouched in silence as the murderers combed the area. Two minutes passed. Five minutes. The two men traced their steps thirty yards beyond the terrified witnesses.

As Eddie dared to look around the rock, he leaned against a dry, birch twig. The snap exploded throughout the woods and Fats wheeled in the dark.

"Run!" Eddie yelled. They flew from their cover like quail from a bird dog.

"Get 'em, Harold!" Fats thundered.

The four raced toward the East Bluff Road. Pete led the way with Dan close behind.

134

"Split up!" Eddie ordered. "Pete, stay with Dan! Head for the fort. Kate, stay with me."

Pete glanced over his shoulder. Thirty yards back Fats and Geetings boiled out of the woods.

"This way, Pete!" Dan motioned, and they raced down the road in front of the East Bluff homes. Geetings was barely twenty-five yards behind and gaining. The thought of Harold Geetings grabbing them and crushing their heads together strengthened each of the boys' strides.

Ahead, under a streetlamp, stood a carriage tied to a hitching post. Dan looked back. Mr. Geetings was now only twenty yards behind. "Jump in, Pete," Dan yelled. Dan grabbed the reins and whacked the nearest horse on his flank. The team began to trot down the gravel road and Dan swung himself onto the rig.

"Hey," a man yelled out from the other side of the gate. "That's the Governor's carriage."

Dan landed in the driver's seat yelling, "Geddup!" He grabbed a whip and put it to use. The old man was closing fast—ten yards, five yards. He reached for a handhold just as the horses felt the sting of Dan's whip. The team caught stride and raced toward the fort. Pete looked back to see Mr. Geetings standing in the moonlight shaking his fists.

Dan slowed the team to a trot directing them behind the fort and past the Governor's mansion. "We're safe, at least for the moment," he said.

Dan decided to leave the rig at the Grand Hotel Snack Bar so it might look like one of the hotel guests had taken it as a practical joke. That would give the policeman, old Jack Chamberlain, something to do for the next few days, interrogating a thousand indignant tourists at the insistence of the Governor of Michigan.

Pete and Dan ran in the shadows down to the boardwalk.

"Let's get to the *Griffin*." Dan said.

"Why don't we go to your uncle's place?" Pete asked.

"If Fats recognized Kate or me, he'd know we'd be staying with Aunt and Uncle. He could be on his way to the west bluff right now. If we showed up there, we'd never make it inside."

"What happens if Kate and Eddie weren't as lucky as we were?" Pete asked. "What if Fats got 'em?"

"I don't know," Dan sighed. "We just have to do what Eddie told us and hope they got away."

The two hurried past the Windermere Hotel. The town was lit up as bright as day with a hundred gaslights all along Huron Avenue. The streets and sidewalks were bustling with people, bikes, and horses. Pete walked in the shadows thinking about what Fats had done to Cahill. He looked out across the harbor, the moon glistening on the bay. He looked at Dan. "Is she okay?"

"Please?" Dan replied, absently.

"Is Kate all right?" Pete repeated. "You can tell, can't you?"

"Usually, yes. But I've got this odd feeling. I think we'd better be ready to sail," he said glancing at the clouds flying in from the west.

The two boys waited under the coal dock ten yards from the *Griffin*. Five minutes passed. Ten.

"I'm sorry," Pete whispered. "I couldn't help it."

"It wasn't your fault, Pete," Dan replied. "I'm just surprised I didn't throw up first."

———

"This way, Kate," Eddie called as they raced out from Robinson's Folly Trail. He knew Fats was right behind; he could feel the earth shake.

Eddie'd known for years that the twins had an uncanny knack for recognizing when the other was in a pinch. Two summers ago, Dan broke his leg when he followed a porcupine into the swamp a mile back behind his cottage. Kate and Eddie were swimming with several friends near their boathouse. Suddenly Kate stopped and stared toward shore. She grabbed Eddie by his arm, "Something's wrong with Danny," she shrieked. They both raced to shore, threw on some shoes, and charged into the woods. Eddie followed as Kate crashed through the brush, over fallen logs and around huge rocks. When they found Dan, he was unconscious, lying beside a pine stump, his leg pointing awkwardly into the air. Eddie scooped him up and rushed him back to the cottage where Dr. Hinken set the break. Even at that, Dan nearly didn't make it.

———

The four ran headlong out from Robinson's Folly when Eddie made his decision. Knowing Dan and Kate's sixth sense for finding each other, he split them up. He sent Pete with Dan toward the fort and led Kate toward Arch Rock. He and Kate would be sure to find bicycles along the road left by people having parties on the bluff. As they raced for their lives, Eddie turned to see Fats slowly losing ground.

"Kate, grab a bike. We'll lose him for good."

It was one of those good ideas that doesn't work. Eddie and Kate jumped on a couple of two-wheelers and raced along the trail. Unfortunately, Fats found a bike, as well, and immediately gained ground on them. It soon became evident that he could overtake them any time he wished. Instead of following them, he was, in reality, directing them deeper into the woods. He was so close that if they tried to dump their bikes and make a run for it off the trail, he could easily drive at least one of them into the ground. But he didn't want just one. He wanted to finish both of them right then.

"I think he's trying to push us inland," Eddie panted.

"You're right," Kate puffed. "This road leads to the north end of the island. If he catches us there, we won't have a chance."

"We've got to head back toward town," Eddie gasped as they neared Arch Rock.

"I've got an idea, Eddie. Follow me."

With a burst of speed, she shot past Eddie and, as they entered the large Carriage Tours turn-around, they pedaled toward Sugar Loaf Road with Fats still twenty yards behind.

"Here we go," Kate said. Instead of staying on the bike path, she whipped a 180 and buzzed past the startled dockmaster. He reached out to grab her, but she swerved and he missed. Fats lost his balance and nearly fell as he reached for Eddie. The dockmaster regained control of his bike and spun around. He had lost valuable seconds but he wasn't out of the chase.

Downhill they raced toward town. Experience and gravity favored Fats, but youth and fear kept Kate and Eddie just out of his reach. Five minutes later, the three flew past Ste. Anne's Church into the outskirts of the village, Eddie and Kate ahead by twenty yards. They pedalled ferociously past the yacht dock and Father Marquette Park. As they careened into town they began to dodge people, bikes, and horses.

When they reached Betty's Gifts, Kate looked up and saw a black, Grand Hotel dray turning slowly onto the Arnold Dock. She swerved grazing a horse's nose. Eddie veered to the right just missing the end of the wagon. The immense draught horses spooked, rearing their heads and neighing furiously.

The driver lost control and his team charged up the street heading directly toward Fats. The dockmaster found himself staring straight into the wild-eyed faces of two frantic, runaway Percherons and a panic-stricken teamster.

Fats stood on his brakes, immediately spinning out. He and his bicycle parted company in mid-air. The bike slid under the wagon and was crushed by its wide, steel-rimmed wheels. Fats flew toward the curb landing face first in a large mound of mooshy, horse manure. He bounced up, swearing a blue streak trying to clear his eyes.

By the time he had, Eddie and Kate were gone.

———

Chief Chamberlain sat at his Market Street police desk having a career night on the telephone. Calls poured in from all over the island:

"You're at a pay phone where? . . . Arch Rock? . . . Three bikes were stolen. . . . All right. Two kids first and then a fat guy. Are you sure? . . . Okay, I'll watch for them. . . .

"You're calling for the Governor? Yes, I'll hold. . . . Yes, Governor. . . . Someone has stolen your carriage? . . . Right, sir. I'll get right on it. . . . Yes, sir, . . . No respect at all, sir."

"Hurry," came the next call. "There's a runaway dray. People and horses are scattered everywhere . . ."

139

". . . I'd like to report four house guests missing from our residence on the West Bluff."

"You'll have to get in line, lady," Jack Chamberlain responded. "All hell's breaking loose in town. I can't be looking for strays right now. . . . Oh, Nancy, it's you. All right. I'll watch for them. . . . Teenagers, you say, three boys and a girl? Right. You want my advice? Put some food out. Hamburgers. French fries. They'll be back before you know it with a dozen others just like 'em. I've seen it happen."

———

After seeing Fats fall from his bike, Eddie and Kate never looked back until they were beyond the Iroquois Hotel.

"We lost him, Kate," Eddie gasped as he coasted around the bend. They leaned the bikes against the fence in front of the Cawthorn mansion.

"We'd better get to the *Griffin*," Kate said.

"The wind is picking up," Eddie noticed. "Check out those clouds to the west."

"Oh, no," Kate said as she glanced up and saw the triangular, red flag flying stiffly from the Coast Guard station yardarm. "Small craft warnings. We've got to hurry. I hope Dan and Pete are waiting for us at the *Griffin*. I don't know about you, Eddie, but I want to get off this island."

"Me, too," Eddie said. "Fats and Geetings will turn this place upside down to find us. There aren't any ferry boats traveling this late at night so maybe they won't think to watch the harbor. The *Griffin* is our only chance."

"Let's go," Kate said. "The way the moon is popping in and out from behind the clouds, we might not have any light to rig her."

CHAPTER 27
ESCAPE

10:30 p.m.

"There she is," Kate whispered as the moon broke through the rocky shoreline onto the *Griffin*.

"Hold it, Kate." Eddie grabbed her arm and they dropped to their knees behind the beached sailboat. "Someone's coming from the coal dock."

As Pete and Dan approached the *Griffin*, Dan called softly, "Eddie, Kate, is that you?"

"Oh, Dan," Kate said, standing up. "I just knew you'd make it. Are you all right?"

"We're fine," Dan assured her. "Come on. We're going to cast off and make a run for it. With this wind, we should reach the Snows before dawn."

"You read my mind, Dan," Eddie said. "Let's go."

The four pushed the sailboat, stern first, into the water. Eddie hopped aboard, unlocked the door to the cabin, and tossed the sail bags and stays onto the deck. The four worked furiously getting the *Griffin* rigged for a midnight sail.

141

Eddie tossed the paddle to Pete. "Spin her around, Pete. Keep the bow pointed into the wind."

Kate set the jib and Dan ran the centerboard down into position.

"Hoist the main, Dan," Eddie directed. Up she went, and they were off. The full moon broke through the clouds just as Eddie began to steer his course along the west breakwall.

"Ready about!" Eddie ordered as he watched a black cloud approach the full moon. He waited several moments, then called, "Hard alee!" and spun the tiller to his right. The wind popped the mainsail and the boom shot over the ducked heads of his crew. The *Griffin* raced through the pitch black bay toward the safety of the east breakwall. As she blew across the harbor, the moon broke momentarily from its cover and shone brilliantly on the *Griffin*, practically shouting to everyone on shore, "Here are the four kids who are trying to escape from the two murderers and the corrupt policeman. Somebody, run and tell the bad guys!"

Young couples, chilled by the night air, comforted each other in their blankets along the shore and were treated to the spectacular sight of a small boat under full sail in the bright moonlight.

Fortunately, Fats and Geetings were inland searching Mackinac Island's hiding places and were too busy to notice the *Griffin* making her escape. She flew out of sight behind the east breakwall and then into the open Straits water beyond Mission Point.

With his small flashlight, Eddie set the compass for an east-by-northeast run to the Les Cheneaux Islands. At the same time, a monstrous thunderhead raced directly into the *Griffin's* path, its captain and crew unaware of a peril more devastating and even less forgiving than the combined wrath of Harold Geetings and Fats FitzRoberts.

11:30 p.m.

The barometer at the Coast Guard station had been dropping steadily all evening. At midnight the commander ordered the officer on duty to raise a second triangular flag. The weather service had upgraded the storm to a full gale with winds expected to reach sixty miles per hour.

———

Once out from the lee of Mackinac Island, Eddie noticed, not only was the wind getting stronger, but it was shifting to the south. Earlier that evening it had been moderate and from the west, perfect for a fast sail back to the Snows. He suspected now that the *Griffin* was in for a major storm.

The gusts grew stronger for the next two hours and the *Griffin* hydroplaned across the choppy Straits water. By 1:30 a.m., she was already halfway to the Les Cheneaux Islands. They were making record time. Slowly the wind swung further around and raged straight from the east, almost dead on the *Griffin's* nose. The black waves piled higher and the violent gale blew stronger by the minute.

"What are we going to do, Eddie?" Kate hollered, straining to be heard over the shrieking wind.

"I'll keep her on course as long as I can," Eddie shouted, "but she can't take much more pounding. We'll either have to tack or drop sail. If we tack, we might smash on the rocks to the north or be plowed over by a freighter to the south. We're in too much water to drop a hook. There's no telling where we'd end up by the time the storm clears."

Then Eddie recognized another option. "I've got it," he called out. "We'll run for cover behind Goose Island. Kate, tend the jib. Dan, get ready to jibe. Pete, grab something and hold on. Here we go."

Eddie turned the tiller just as lightning exploded on the eastern horizon. Eddie glanced up. In the eerie flash, he noticed the topmost batton had ripped a gaping hole in the main sail. If the seam didn't hold, that would be the end. In this wind, he could never navigate with just the jib. The *Griffin* flew to the northeast, the sails straining at their halyards.

What had been occasional flashes of lightning in the distance soon became nearer and more frequent. The sailors could see Goose Island as easily as though it were a clear, July afternoon. They watched in terror for rocks off the unfamiliar coast as the *Griffin* flew almost out of control toward the uninhabited island.

And then the rains came.

One minute, Goose Island was clearly visible straight off the bow. The next, it was obliterated by a torrential downpour. The deluge was complete, the sky so black that Eddie, from his place at the tiller, couldn't have found his left hand with his right. Still, he kept his course.

Rain poured into the *Griffin* by the barrel. It ripped at the sailors' faces and soaked every stitch of their clothes. The temperature plummeted and they shuddered on the icy deck.

Finally, although unsure of his exact position, Eddie noticed a lessening in the force of the waves and realized he must be in the lee of Goose Island. Going further would surely drive the tiny craft onto a rock sending all aboard to a certain death. He yelled out over the din, "Drop anchor, Dan! Kate, bring in the main. Pete, take in the jib. Cover up, everyone. Get below. Fast!"

The anchor rope screamed from the bow hatch like the line off Pete's fishing reel. Almost immediately, it slackened as the hook hit bottom. They couldn't be in any more than six feet of water. Dan paid out another hundred feet of line before snubbing it to the bow cleat. The *Griffin's* nose snapped straight into the wind. The four storm-tossed sailors secured the hatches and raced below, latching the cabin door behind them.

Dan grabbed the bilge pump and began hand-pumping water from the hold. Eddie lit a lantern and the four sailors bounced in the tight quarters amidst soggy sail bags and cold life jackets.

It was two a.m. No one had slept for eighteen hours—no one, except for Pete who had napped all the way from the Snows to Mackinac that morning. So, qualified or not, Pete was assigned the task of pumping the bilge and awakening Eddie in case something worse happened.

"Worse? Like what?" Pete mumbled. Nobody heard him and he didn't really want to know.

Completely exhausted, his friends fell quickly into a fitful sleep. Pumping the bilge wasn't glamorous work, but, as Eddie explained, it was better than looking up in the morning through a hundred feet of water.

Hasty Departure

CHAPTER 28
THE WRITER

Monday, June 30 5:00 a.m.

Ever so slowly, the pitch black of the stormy night became the gray of dawn. Fats and Harold began to distinguish the outlines of trees and the peaks of churches. Through the long, rainy hours of darkness they had searched every natural and man-made shelter from Skull Cave to Devil's Kitchen. Their eyes stung and every muscle ached. It had been a dreadfully wet, bone-wearying job, but they had to catch those miserable kids before they could either escape from the island or find help on it.

"Okay," Fats said to Harold as the sun broke the horizon, "I'll stay in town. The only way those little brats can get away is by boat, and no boat can come or go from this island without me knowing it. Now, listen good, old man. You've got to go about your business like nothing's happened. But keep your eyes peeled. You see anything, you call me, understand?"

146

The old writer nodded and went wearily to Fats' room. He dressed quickly for his appearances. The first book-signing was scheduled for ten a.m. at the library on Market Street. After that, he would have a press conference on George and Nancy Anderson's summer home porch. From there, he would be escorted to the Grand Hotel lobby where hundreds of eager book buyers would shower him with adoration. This was Harold Geetings' special day. He had dreamed of it all his life. Unfortunately for him, four little warts had ruined it all.

He boarded a carriage taking him to the library. It was a scene he had rehearsed practically all his adult life. He would receive the people cordially but would speak softly and with a touch of mystery befitting a famous author.

———

As his carriage bumped along the street, he thought back to last summer when it all began. He met Fats at a party at George and Nancy's summer home. It was early in June. They wanted to help him with his book, *Les Cheneaux Lovers*, by introducing him to their influential acquaintances. One of them might have a connection with a publisher. Fats, the marina dockmaster by day, had been hired by George Anderson to be bartender for the fancy soiree. Harold was uneasy in the presence of the Andersons' successful friends so he struck up a conversation with the portly bartender. Soon Fats and he were the best of buddies. Harold divulged his entire life story, including how desperately broke he was. He learned that Fats had friends in some sort of printing business. They might like to help Harold. Fats was particularly interested in knowing all about Harold's little island in the Snows, how isolated, yet how near it was to Mackinac.

Fats also asked about Harold's book. Well, Harold practically told him the whole plot. The story, a romance with his Les Cheneaux friends as its principal characters, had been turned down by every publisher in the country. It was a great novel, Harold assured Fats, a surefire best seller, certainly better than the trash he'd seen lately in the book stores.

Two days later, Fats approached Harold as he walked by the yacht dock. "Listen," Fats said, "I called my friends and told them about you. They may have a way for you to make some money this summer."

"Really?" Harold replied eagerly. "What would I do? How much would I earn?"

Fats hesitated a moment. "You do just like you're told, you'd get thirty thousand dollars," Fats said slowly.

"Thirty thousand?" Harold questioned. "For three months' work? It's not illegal, is it? Who are your friends?"

"Well, Harold, we're not talking charity work here and they're not exactly the local Rotary Club," he glowered at the old man. "But it's only for one summer. We do our jobs right, there's no risk. I'm offering you a way out of a real jam, Harold. Another winter on that little island of yours without cash and you're a dead man. Suppose you go back to your cabin and think it over. I'll meet you there in a couple days."

Two days later, Fats came to Harold's island in the Snows. He looked around Elliot Bay at all the small cottages and the two quiet hotels. It was a bit backward for his tastes but it was perfect for their plans. Fats docked his boat next to Harold's old outboard and ushered himself inside the cabin. He sat down at the old man's kitchen table and wasted no time explaining the operation. Harold listened, his eyes cast down to the floor. He knew Fats was right. He had no choice. He agreed to Fats' proposition.

The next week, Harold received several small, heavy boxes in the mail. When they had all arrived, Fats and he opened them and assembled the compact but sturdily built printing press. They also received one hundred sheets of paper smuggled by the mob from the United States Bureau of Engraving. They were interspersed among the pages of two dozen otherwise useless textbooks. Fats and Harold cut them from the binding. That night, they printed six hundred replicas of a United States of America twenty dollar bill, $12,000 in fake currency.

A few days later, Fats received the seed money to open a bike rental which he set up near the Mackinac Island yacht dock. Everything was in place by June 15th. Harold's job was to sit at the rental booth collecting a twenty-five dollar deposit for each of the one hundred bicycles. As each bike was returned at the end of the day, Harold would keep five dollars for rent and give the customer a counterfeit twenty for the rest of the deposit. Harold was careful to give only one fake bill to a family. It wouldn't do to have two of them in the hands of someone who might notice the identical serial numbers. Since most of the tourists returned their bikes just before leaving the island, they'd rush to the rental stand, settle up with Harold, board the ferry, and leave the island.

For each twelve thousand dollars printed, Fats and Harold each cleared a thousand for themselves.

The mob got the rest. Fats and Harold also split the bike rental proceeds. Every ten days Fats mailed the mob their cut in real twenties and they would send Harold two more cases of books to the Cedarville Post Office. On the night before a shipment was due, Fats would take Harold on a midnight spin over to Harold's cabin on the new, Italian-built speedboat. Fats would drop Harold off at his dock and return to Mackinac the same night. Harold would go into town the next morning in his old outboard and get the boxes of books from the post office. He'd cut out the paper and print the counterfeit currency that afternoon in his cabin. Fats would pick him up sometime after midnight and they'd return to Mackinac. Unless there was a storm, they'd never miss a day at the bike stand and the speedboat would never appear to be moved from its slip at the yacht dock. The whole summer passed without a hitch. It was as slick a counterfeit scheme as any ever devised.

Just after Labor Day as Fats and Harold were storing the bicycles under the Island House porch, Fats received a phone call. It seemed that they had done their jobs so well that the New York investors wanted another year out of the scam. Fats told Harold and Harold flew into a rage. He wouldn't do it. Fats calmly explained that the message was not so much an invitation as it was a demand. Harold had no choice, not if he had any plans for the rest of his life.

Harold returned to the Snows that fall with more money than he'd ever had. He bought a new typewriter and provisions for the entire winter. He tried to drown himself in his old manuscripts but he soon found the old plots and characters were somehow unrealistic. He dwelt on nothing but his seemingly insoluable dilemma. It wouldn't go away and every day brought him closer to next summer's torture. Then, one blazingly bright, January day, Harold seized upon an idea. He'd write his story as though it were fiction. He pounded out 160 pages in less than a month. He called it *Mackinac Passage* although he had no intention of ever submitting it to a publisher. It would be his passage from Mackinac to freedom. Once again, however, even in his own story, Harold proved to be a failure; he couldn't think of even one practical conclusion that would resolve his predicament.

By the middle of February, Harold was totally frustrated. To eliminate it from his every waking thought, he wrote a somewhat plausible conclusion and mailed the entire manuscript to the most prominent publishing house in the country. He'd never hear from it again. "Good riddance," he mumbled as he handed it to Archie Visnaw at the post office.

March and April passed quickly as he immersed himself once again in *Les Cheneaux Lovers*, but May weighed heavily on his mind. At midnight on June 1st, he heard the familiar drone of an approaching speedboat. Fats had come to Harold's island to make the passage together over to Mackinac.

They stayed the night at Fats' Crews Quarters room and were joined the next morning at the bike booth by Joey Cahill, a tall, skinny young man with a strong, almost unintelligible, East Coast accent. Harold was hopeful that Cahill had been sent to take his place or, better still, put an end to the whole counterfeit scheme. Instead, Joey had been sent to speed things up. "Da boys back East t'ink youse ain't doin' yer job so good. Dey want you should double da take, see?" is how he explained his presence.

Well, Joey sped things up, all right. He also infuriated Fats by constantly referring to him as "da fatso boat boy." He took over the afternoon shift at the bike booth and gave a fake twenty to every returning customer. Almost immediately, problems began. Early in June, the Mackinac Island policeman, Jack Chamberlain, got a call from Larry Perel, the Iroquois Hotel manager who reported that two identical twenties were in his night's receipts. The policeman asked a few questions and soon realized that both of the fake bills had come from the bike rental by the yacht dock. Jack Chamberlain watched the operation for two days and, instead of arresting Fats, Harold, and Joey, he struck a deal with them. For $250 a day, he would cover their mistakes and keep secret any further reports.

Then a very strange thing happened. Harold Geetings was visited by James Barnwell, the president of the publishing company in California where he'd sent his manuscript in February. *Mackinac Passage* had not only been accepted for publication, but its rights had been sought by a large motion picture company. Harold was flabbergasted. *Mackinac Passage* was the worst thing he'd ever written. He hadn't even proofed it! But there it was. A check for twenty thousand dollars and a promise from Mr. Barnwell that the movie contract would be for much, much more. Harold would be rich.

He told Fats that he wanted out of the counter-feit scam. Fats insisted that he had no choice but to finish the summer. Then, three days later, Joey

Cahill used five of the counterfeit twenties for dinner and drinks at the Lamplighter Dining Room at the Murray Hotel. Two employees noticed the bills and mentioned it to the editor of the *Town Crier* who happened to be dining there. By the time Jack Chamberlain could cover it up, the newspapers had already gone to press.

Well, Fats didn't agonize very long deciding what to do about Joey. Even though Harold had tried, he knew it was no use. Fats was going to do away with the skinny punk. They might have gotten away with it, too, if it hadn't been for those four kids that happened along at the wrong time.

———

The carriage pulled up to the library bringing Harold to his first engagement. He stepped from the carriage looking like a shining example of the Great American Dream. Instead, he was the victim of greed and a most despicable scheme. His only chance to extricate himself from the firm grip of the mob lay in the distasteful assignment of catching and eliminating four witnesses to a crime he not only did not commit, but tried to prevent. However, unless he helped Fats cover up Cahill's murder, he knew he would be judged guilty just as surely as though he had bashed Joey's head in himself.

Harold left the library at 11:30. He boarded a black Grand Hotel carriage that escorted him to the West Bluff residence of his friends, George and Nancy Anderson. The one-horse brougham rolled up to the Anderson's home with great fanfare. Newsreel cameras, photographers, and journalists captured the whole event for the world to see. Harold signed the movie contract for fifty thousand dollars. He was then invited inside by the lovely Mrs. Anderson.

The front door closed and Nancy practically wilted into a cushioned, wicker chair. "Oh, Harold," she said immediately, "we're so worried."

"What's wrong, Nancy?" Harold asked.

"George and I have been up all night," she replied. "My niece and nephew and two other boys came to visit us yesterday and now they've vanished. George is out looking for them right now."

Harold knew immediately he'd hit pay dirt.

"They sailed here from their cabins in the Snows," Nancy continued, fighting off tears. "They visit us several times each summer. Last night, after dinner, they went to the yacht dock for a party assuring us they would be back before dark. It's not like them to do this. I telephoned Chief Chamberlain last night. He was too busy then so I called again this morning, but he said the Governor needed him for some special investigation at the Grand. Oh, Harold, I have no one to turn to."

As Nancy began to weep openly, Harold Geetings' mind was racing. Everything was falling into place. He remembered now. It was Cedarville. That's where he'd seen the scruffy, brown-haired boy before. He was forever getting in his way—at the post office—in the channel—at the grocery. And the other three. He knew who they were, too. They were the ones from Cincinnati Row that were always cutting in front of his outboard in their mahogany sailboat. They had been spying on him that day on the Cedarville dock. "Good Deed Club," hah! They were probably the ones Fats saw racing away from his cabin that day when he had gone into town for a paper shipment. They must have come to Mackinac in their sailboat yesterday afternoon and then, last night, they trailed him up to the East Bluff and watched Fats scramble Joey's brains.

Harold listened eagerly to Nancy for any clue that might lead him to where they were hiding. Suddenly, it dawned on him. They weren't on the island at all. They'd left during the night on their sailboat.

"You know, Nancy, I might be able to help," Harold began anxiously. "I remember seeing four teenagers, three boys and a girl, last night. I heard them say they were going to ride their bikes out to the north end to show their friend the crack in the island. I didn't give it any thought at the time, but there are two cracks and both of them are very dangerous. I'll call my friend, Gerald FitzRoberts, at the yacht dock. He'll ride out and search the area around one of the cracks and I'll check the other. If you have a bicycle, I could go directly from here. It will be faster than taking a carriage."

"Oh, Harold, would you?" Nancy Anderson exclaimed. "But your autograph session at the Grand," she remembered, "I can't have you miss your appearance. It's too important to you."

"Not nearly as important as your niece and nephew are to you," the old man replied. "Hurry along now. You get the bike while I telephone Gerald. We'll have those kids rounded up in no time."

Arch Rock —

CHAPTER 29
FOUND

Noon

Fats rocked uneasily on his porch chair exhausted from the all-night search. He rested the binoculars on his chest after, once again, scanning the Arnold Transit pier. Another passenger ferry had just cast off from the east side of the dock for its return trip to Mackinaw City. Once again, no one remotely resembling the four kids had boarded. Where could they be?

The telephone rang inside his room. On the third ring, Fats rocked forward in his chair. He stepped into his quarters and picked up the receiver, "Yacht dock, FitzRoberts."

"Fire up the speedboat, Gerald." It was the old man. "I'll be aboard in ten minutes."

"Harold, what's happened?" Fats demanded.

"I've got 'em. Or at least I know where they are. I'm up at the Andersons' on the west bluff. The kids we chased last night? Two of them are relatives of George and Nancy. Listen carefully. The

Andersons know nothing about what's happened except that their guests are missing. The kids sailed here from Cedarville yesterday and must have beached their boat rather than tying it up at the yacht dock. I know all four of them, Fats. They live within a mile of my cabin, one almost right outside my door. My guess is they've been playing detective and figured out the whole counterfeit scheme. They came here to prove it, but when they saw what happened to Cahill, they got scared and made a run for the Snows. That's why you never saw them leave this morning. They slipped out last night. Probably before the storm. Normally it wouldn't take very long for them to make the crossing, five, maybe six hours. But if I'm right, we still have a chance. Get the boat ready. I'll be right there."

Fats slammed the receiver onto the hook. He grabbed his 30-06 hunting rifle and a box of cartridges. He wrapped them in a blanket and stuffed a stack of counterfeit twenties in his jacket pocket as he charged out the door. He strode down the dock to the speedboat, ripped off the black canvas tarp, and jumped aboard. He flipped the mooring lines from their pilings leaving only two short dock lines tied to their cleats. He turned the blower on and checked the lake conditions. Looking back ashore he noticed that two limp, red triangular flags were being brought down from the yardarm at the Coast Guard station.

That was it! That's why Harold said they still had a chance! The kids were on a small sailboat. The trip to the Snows might only take a few hours— under normal conditions. But last night, a gale passed through the Straits. The winds were too strong for a small boat to sail. They would have to find shelter or be blown out of the water. And to-day the winds had died. They'd be becalmed. A sailboat without an auxiliary motor would be stranded—dead in the water until the weather changed. If Harold knew these kids, he must also know that their boat was not equipped with an emergency engine. What a break for Fats and Harold! What rotten luck for those little brats. If the storm didn't blow their sailboat apart last night, Fats would do the job with his rifle real soon.

Fats smiled as he turned the key. The whole job wouldn't take an hour, round trip. The water gurgled softly off the stern. Fats searched Fort Street alongside Doud's Grocery. Harold should be along any second. "Come on, you old grizzly," Fats said under his breath.

He unwrapped the long, blue blanket on the floor and withdrew the rifle. He loaded it with five cartridges and set it out of sight along the star-board gunwale.

"There you are," Fats muttered seeing Harold coasting down the steep hill. "Let's go, old man."

Harold cruised past the Coast Guard station before slowing to a stop at the marina. He jumped off the bike and marched out onto the pier.

"Hurry it up, Geetings," Fats hissed as Harold approached the last slip. The old man undid the two dock lines and stepped aboard. Fats eased the gear shift forward and the speedboat moved slowly into the harbor. He glanced in all directions looking for any traffic that might get in his way. He set his sights on the Snows and slammed the throttle ahead.

The black-hulled speedboat thundered around the east breakwall and was gone in a heartbeat.

CHAPTER 30
THE *GRIFFIN*

Monday, June 30 3:00 a.m.

Throughout the night, the *Griffin* bounced in the Straits buffeted by torrential rain squalls. She was a day-sailer built for afternoon excursions or short-course regattas. The area below deck provided storage for her sails and gear. Period. This night, however, four weary, bone-cold sailors huddled here among soggy sail bags and lumpy life jackets.

Lightning flashes illuminated the tiny cabin and thunder claps made sleep for Kate, Dan, and Eddie fitful at best.

Pete, however, the appointed sentry, was catatonic with fear. He couldn't blink, let alone sleep. There he was, cramped below on a fifty-year-old, wooden sailboat anchored in the middle of the Straits of Mackinac, an area revered by hard-hat divers around the world as some sort of shipwreck mecca. Steel freighters, seven hundred feet long some of them, eighteenth and nineteenth century

159

schooners, assorted merchant ships, naval vessels and luxury yachts had met their doom within hailing distance of the *Griffin.* Pete's friends' twenty-five foot long wooden sloop was being held in place by a hundred feet of 3/8 inch hemp line, kite string under even the best of conditions.

And the night was like pitch. Between lightning bolts, Pete's stomach was having a hard time telling whether he was right-side-up or upside-down. His most immediate concern, however, was not the frailty of the boat. Neither was it the force of the storm nor the darkness of the night. Pete sat transfixed at his station knowing that two desperate murderers could approach silently in their speedboat and blast a hundred rounds through the *Griffin's* thin, wooden hull. Their objective met, they could spin around and return to Mackinac harbor before the small boat had even begun to bump along in her final resting place at the bottom of the Straits, her four, bullet-ridden crewmembers trapped in the small cabin forever. No, Pete didn't think he'd have any trouble keeping guard that night.

But by three a.m. the rain stopped. By four, the wind had died and the waves started to rock the *Griffin* in a soft, rolling manner. Pete grew drowsy and began to imagine that, perhaps, the rotund dockmaster and the elderly writer might not really care any more about the four youths they had followed earlier that night. Besides, the two old men were probably tired and would need to sleep. Need to sleep . . . s l e e p . . . s l e e p . . .

———

The pre-dawn light awakened Eddie. He peeked through the starboard porthole to see the southern shore of Goose Island. He was immediately relieved that the *Griffin* hadn't drifted during the night, but suddenly, he realized the wind had completely died. He was instantly reminded of a previous sail. One that he and Dan would never forget.

Last year, coming back from Mackinac, Eddie and Dan miraculously survived a white squall, a brief but intense wind storm common in the tropics but rare in the Great Lakes. Summer storms, as ore boat captains call them, strike without warning. They come right out of the blue and blast a few square miles of open water with gusts up to one hundred miles per hour. They might last as little as five minutes but can flip large yachts upside down or snatch a napping deckhand from a freighter's hatch. Then, just as suddenly, they're gone.

The *Griffin* had somehow been spared the worst of the white squall's fury, but less than an hour later, it was subjected to another weather condition almost as devastating. The *Griffin* had been becalmed.

If a white squall isn't the worst thing that can happen to a small sailboat, then drifting in the middle of a boundless sea with one hundred degree temperatures certainly is. There had not been the slightest breath of wind that August afternoon. Just stifling heat, blazing sun, and constant glare. The boys took turns helping each other in and out of the water just to keep from roasting on the deck. The *Griffin* had remained motionless for an hour. For two hours. Six hours. In the twelfth hour, an evening breeze lifted the sails of the *Griffin* and Eddie, sunburned and exhausted, guided her home.

Dr. Hinken hadn't mentioned this possibility to Pete's dad for one reason. Dr. Hinken hadn't known about it. He had never even been told about Dan and Eddie's escapade to Mackinac, let alone the fact that the two adventurers had survived a white squall and then been becalmed. The boys had gone to Mackinac without their parents' permission. They each told their parents that they were taking the *Griffin* to camp out overnight in nearby Duck Bay as they'd often done before. Instead, they sailed to Mackinac to introduce themselves to the girls working at the various hotels and restaurants. They'd stay the night on the beach and return to the Snows the next day. But the return trip last year had taken sixteen hours.

———

Eddie jumped to his feet and shook Dan by the shoulder. As soon as Dan opened his eyes, he recognized the problem.

"Rollers," Dan muttered nervously. What he saw were the remnant waves of a storm that serve only to cause seasickness to a becalmed sailboat's crew.

The seriousness of the situation immediately sharpened the sailors' senses. Each detected a very faint but usable breeze approaching from the south. Their race to the Snows had to be continued immediately. They scrambled from the tiny cabin up to the deck.

———

The sun wasn't even up and Pete's dad was trying to awaken him. He was dangling a big northern from a stringer in front of Pete's nose, waving it back and forth, . . . back and forth, . . . back and forth . . . .

"Pete!" Kate was shaking his shoulder. "Wake up!"

"I'll just sleep in this morning, Dad," Pete mumbled.

"Come on, Pete," she nudged him again.

He bolted up. "Kate, what are you doing here? Where are we?"

"Get up, Pete," Kate urged. "We need your help."

Pete, still clenching the bilge pump, shook himself out of his makeshift bed and hurried topside.

"Bring in the anchor, Pete," Dan said anxiously. "I'll set the jib. The main sail was ripped worse than we thought. Two battons are missing and it's barely holding at the seam."

As the sun rose, a breath of air passed over the Straits. Eddie raced to the tiller as the gentle breeze slowly filled the *Griffin's* jib and damaged main sail. She moved steadily away from the lee of Goose Island. Kate tensed herself near the jib halyard and Dan stood by the main sail. The breeze continued for an hour and the *Griffin* struggled over the Straits water toward the Snows.

Then, with Middle Entrance a mile away and in plain view, the wind died. Eddie, Kate, and Dan remained at their stations while Pete sat idly by without even a rope to hold.

An hour passed.

"How about if I start paddling?" Pete offered.

"Go ahead, Pete. It might not help much, but it can't hurt," Eddie replied.

Pete went below, grabbed the paddle, and eased himself forward along the deck. Straddling the bow, Pete quickly became absorbed in a steady, rowing rhythm. He remembered a sea chantey that Ann Early had sung at a campfire one night along the shore of Cincinnati Row. As Ann had done that evening, Pete adapted the old song to fit the occasion. He began quietly, to himself,

163

The main sail is up and the anchor's aweigh,
Away, Cheneaux,
We're home for the Snows and we'll be there today,
And we're bound for the Les Cheneaux.

As Pete began the chorus, Dan joined in with his best, octave-below-normal, piratey voice:

It's away, Cheneaux,
High away, Les Cheneaux,
We're home for the Snows and we'll be there today,
And we're bound for the Les Cheneaux.

A soft breeze resumed from the west, not enough to fill the sails completely, but it did provide hope. Pete continued to paddle. Now everyone was busy and spirits soared. If the breeze held out, the *Griffin* would fly through Middle Entrance, around Reif's Point and be home in less than an hour.

On the other hand, if it failed, they could be sitting ducks floating on a mill pond waiting for Fats and Mr. Geetings to blow them to Kingdom Come. They tried not to speculate on the latter possibility.

Dan, instead, had been working on a new verse:

The west wind will blow us to Cedarville Bay,
Away, Cheneaux,
We'll each down a 'Mud' in the Bon Air today,
And we're bound for the Les Cheneaux.

When they'd done the chorus, Eddie grinned, "I got one."

Old Fats, he fell plop from his bike in horse poop,
Away, Cheneaux,
He skidded along like a greasy old sloop,
And we're bound for the Les Cheneaux.

A light breeze kept them going to the mouth of Middle Entrance, but then, once again, it stopped. They sat anxiously, gazing intently at the horizon. Dan went below and returned quickly, "I'd forgotten about these binoculars," he said as he cleaned the lenses and adjusted the focus. The *Griffin* sat dead in the water, her mainsail was limp and her and jib flopped from side to side in the rollers.

"I'm going up the mast and see if I can't get someone's attention," Dan announced. He put the binoculars around his neck and shinnied to the top of the forty foot spar.

"No luck," Dan called down. "No one's out there."

He then worked his way around the mast and focused on a line toward Mackinac Island. A speck of white broke on the blue surface.

White meant waves.

Waves meant a boat.

Dan concentrated on the tiny speck. A fast moving craft was approaching the *Griffin*. He knew intuitively that it was Fats and Geetings. They were maybe ten minutes away.

"I can't say for sure," Dan said sliding down, "but I think Fats is coming this way."

They all spun around and fixed their eyes on the western horizon.

"Pass the binoculars," Eddie said.

The spray turned not one degree from a direct line to the sailboat.

All the while, from the opposite direction, a small outboard powered by an 18-horse, Hiawatha engine chugged up along the shoreline toward the becalmed sailboat. The *Flossy* approached to within twenty yards of the *Griffin*.

"Hey! Pete!" Cara yelled, startling the *Griffin's* crew. They turned to see Pete's big sister.

"I thought you were supposed to be good sailors," Cara taunted. "Can't you go any faster than that?"

"Cara!" Pete replied. "How'd you get here?"

"Well," Cara said as she guided the *Flossy* up to the sailboat, "Dr. Hinken came by this morning and said he'd gotten a call that you kids had skipped breakfast. He said not to worry, but I got to thinking, `Pete? Miss a meal?' I decided to worry. So I came looking for you. Well, do you want me to tow you in or not?"

"No time for that!" Pete yelled. "Dan, drop the *Griffin's* anchor. Everybody, quick, board the *Flossy*."

"Hey, what's going on?" Pete's sister protested. "This isn't the *Queen Mary*, you know."

"I can't explain now," Pete interrupted. "Move over, I'm driving." Everyone hopped aboard the *Flossy* as Pete pulled the starting cord.

"We'll never make it down Middle Entrance before they catch us," Eddie yelled over the whine of the engine.

"I know," Pete said as he slammed the gear forward. He spun the little boat around and headed east along the rocky coast.

"Where are you going?" Kate asked in bewilderment.

"Bosely," Pete called back, setting his jaw.

"Bosely Channel?" she exclaimed. "We'll never get through. It's too shallow. We'll run aground."

"No, we won't," Pete said grimly. "Besides, we don't have much choice. It's two miles down Middle Entrance and only a half mile to Bosely."

Pete reached back and adjusted the lean/rich setting and instantly got another mile-per-hour out of the engine.

"Cara," he said turning to his sister. "You've been through this year. What do you think?"

"Through Bosely?" Cara replied. "Well, yes, once in the tin boat fishing with Dad, but Kate's right. I tilted the motor and we went real slow. Out here in the open water I had to work my way around huge boulders. If we hit a rock at full speed, Pete, the gas tank could split wide open. A spark from the engine would blow us sky high!"

Pete never blinked as he focused straight ahead. He was going way too fast to avoid the rocks but not nearly fast enough to beat Fats to the channel.

The black boat approached the anchored sailboat.

"They're stopping at the *Griffin*," Eddie yelled, looking through the binoculars. "Fats is boarding her. He's kicking in the cabin door. Hold it. He's going back to the speedboat." Eddie stopped his narrative.

"What are they doing?" Kate demanded.

"They're looking down Middle Entrance," Eddie reported hopefully. "Geetings is pointing at something."

"Maybe we should stop here and play possum," Dan said.

"Oh, no." Eddie said. "Fats is turning this way. I think he sees us. Don't slow down now, Pete!"

The little outboard was still three hundred yards from the entrance to Bosely Channel when Fats jammed the throttle ahead and raced toward the *Flossy.*

"Here they come," Eddie warned, bringing the binoculars down to his waist.

"They've got us, Pete," Kate resigned.

As they raced along the shore, Pete watched for the Bosely Channel entrance. He kept the engine at full throttle. The black boat was closing fast and the *Flossy* was still two hundred yards from safety. The big boat was now only twenty yards behind the smaller outboard.

Fats stepped back and turned the steering wheel over to Harold. Harold guided the speed-boat up to within ten yards of the *Flossy* and then eased back on the throttle to match speeds with it.

Fats bent down. He stood up calmly holding a long, wooden object.

"Pete!" Kate screamed. "Fats has a gun!"

Fats leveled his 30-06 at Pete's head as Harold Geetings cruised in for the kill. It was all over.

The Black Hulled Boat

CHAPTER 31
BOSELY CHANNEL

2:00 p.m.

With the exception of Pete, whose hands were clamped to the steering wheel, the passengers of the *Flossy* huddled on the floor clutching each other, their eyes squinting at the oncoming craft.

The black-hulled speedboat was no more than five yards from the *Flossy*. Harold Geetings watched as Fats smiled with one eye squinted and the other focused down the steel barrel. Fats' finger was slowly squeezing the trigger.

Suddenly, Harold jerked the steering wheel hard to the right. At the same time, he pulled back on the throttle.

Fats lurched forward, nearly flying overboard. He bounced off a railing and careened backwards onto the deck. He sprang to his feet screaming at Geetings as the speedboat drifted to a halt.

The *Flossy's* passengers sat up, suddenly hopeful of escape. They watched as Fats grappled with Mr. Geetings. The dockmaster quickly gained advantage and slammed his rifle butt into the old man's head. Harold Geetings slumped to the deck. Fats lifted his partner's limp body over his head and, with one awesome heave, tossed it over the side like so much garbage.

He rushed to the panel and threw the gear control forward and the throttle to full speed.

The scuffle had happened so quickly that the little outboard was still thirty yards from the channel.

Fats raced ahead guiding the speedboat close to the *Flossy's* stern.

Again, the teenagers scrunched to the floor.

Pete glanced behind him. The barrel of Fats' rifle pointed directly into his eyes.

Over the whine of the motor, Pete heard a voice. "Turn!" Dan yelled.

Pete jerked the steering wheel to the left an instant before a deafening blast.

Fats' bullet whizzed past Pete's ear blowing out the *Flossy's* windshield. Her prop grazed a boulder and the engine whined, but the little outboard skimmed into the channel.

The gun was still trained on Pete's head.

Fats squeezed the trigger once again.

Another blast.

Pete rocketed forward, his death grip on the steering wheel keeping him aboard. Black splinters blew past his head. He recoiled into his seat; his elbow knocked the throttle back and cut the engine.

He spun around to see a ball of clear white, hi-octane fuel exploding behind him. The entire entrance of Bosely Channel was being littered from above like flecks of black snow in a glass ball scene.

The five aboard the *Flossy* gaped at the inferno behind them.

The mystery speedboat and its driver had been blown to smithereens.

CHAPTER 32
SURVIVOR

2:03 p.m.

The *Flossy* sat silently in the shallow water, her bow pointing toward the safety of the cottages not far beyond. Pete set the gear to neutral, pulled the cord, and eased her forward through the channel. Then, without a word, he spun the steering wheel, bumped up the RPMs, and pointed her back toward open water.

"What are you doing?" Cara demanded.

"We've got to go back and look for the old man," Pete replied. "He could still be alive."

"Are you're kidding?" his sister yelled. "What if we find him and haul him aboard? He nearly killed us once already!"

"He could have," Pete said. "But he didn't. Fact is, he saved our lives."

"You're right!" Kate said. "Oh, Pete, we've got to hurry."

Pete guided the *Flossy* back through the smoldering Bosely entrance and raced to the area where Fats had thrown the old man overboard.

"There," Kate shouted, pointing ahead. "That's him."

In the rollers straight off the bow, Pete could see a dark shape mostly under water, rising and falling with the waves. In seconds they were alongside the submerging figure. Eddie reached way down over the port gunwale, grabbed Mr. Geetings' collar, and yanked his head out of the water.

The old man vomited and gasped for air. His eyes rolled back. He wasn't dead, but he wasn't far from it.

"Help me pull him aboard," Eddie hollered.

All five grabbed him, nearly flipping the *Flossy*, but somehow managed to haul Mr. Geetings into the boat. He lay in the bottom gagging and looking greener by the moment.

"Who knows artificial respiration?" Kate asked.

"I do," Cara replied, confident now that the old man was incapable of mounting a proper mutiny. "Help me turn him over."

Eddie and Dan rolled Mr. Geetings on his stomach, his feet near the motor and his head toward the bow. Cara checked his mouth for obstructions and began the lifesaving procedure.

"Dan," Pete said, "get out on the bow and watch for rocks. We're going back through Bosely. With all this extra weight, the prop is bound to hit something. Eddie, you'd better get up there with Dan. Maybe we can skim right over the shallow part. If we shear a pin, we'll never make it to a doctor in time."

As Dan directed Pete through the rocky passage, Pete looked for signs of the missing dockmaster, but there wasn't a sign to be seen. Once into Bosely Channel, Pete cranked the *Flossy* up to half-throttle. Then, reaching Urie Bay, he pushed her wide open.

"We'll take him to my father," Kate and Dan said at once.

Pete glanced behind him and, as Cara leaned back, Mr. Geetings began to breathe on his own. Cara was exhausted and didn't look much better than the victim.

The *Flossy* rounded the white stone-marker buoy at Urie Point and made a straight line for Cedarville Channel.

They were still two hundred yards from the red double boathouse when Kate began shouting, "Dad, come down here! Hurry!"

As Pete ran the *Flossy* onto the beach, Dr. Hinken was rushing down the path to meet them.

"Who's this?" he asked.

"It's Mr. Geetings from Elliot Bay, Dad," Dan explained.

"Harold Geetings?" Dr. Hinken asked. "What in the . . ."

"It's a long story," Kate added quickly. "He saved our lives but was thrown out of his boat doing it. By the time we got back to him, he was going down."

"He threw up about a pail of water when we got him aboard," Eddie added. "Pete's sister, Cara, gave him artificial respiration. Since then, he's just been lying on the bottom of the boat. Will he be okay?"

"He's in shock," Dr. Hinken assessed looking at the old man's pupils and checking his pulse. He glanced along the pebbly beach. "We've got to get him inside. Hurry. Dan, Kate, and I on one side and you three on the other. Get a good hold every-one. Ready? Go."

They rushed the water-logged old man up the path to the Hinken's summer home and set him on the thick rug in front of the fireplace. Harold was breathing, but only barely.

"Get two pillows and some blankets, Dan. Kate, bring me my bag," Dr. Hinken directed.

Dan and Kate raced off in opposite directions and returned in seconds. Dr. Hinken propped the old man's feet with the pillows and covered him with the blanket. He opened his black medical kit and grabbed a stethoscope.

"That's about all you can help me with, kids," he said leaning over his patient. "Go find your mother, Kate. She's been worried sick."

"Oh, my heavens. What's happened?" Mrs. Hinken gasped, rushing in from the parlor. "I saw you coming into the dock so I called George and Nancy. They've turned Mackinac Island upside down looking for you. Is everyone okay? Who's this?"

"We're all fine, Mom," Kate replied.

"Oh, thank goodness," Mrs. Hinken said wrapping her arms around her twins. "Your Aunt Nancy was sure you had fallen into some crack in the island. Where were you?" she asked, holding them out at arm's length. "Oh, it doesn't matter now. You're safe," she said as tears ran down her cheeks.

"By the way," Dr. Hinken said, adjusting a pillow under Mr. Geetings' feet, "where's the *Griffin*?"

"Well," Dan replied, "that's part of the story. It's anchored at the mouth of Middle Entrance. We were becalmed in the Straits when Pete's sister came out to tow us back."

Harold Geetings began to shake, his entire body erupting in violent convulsions. Dr. Hinken reached into his bag and grabbed two vials and a syringe. "Everyone out. Now."

175

"I'll stay and help your father," Ann Hinken said. "It would be best if you didn't interrupt him for a while. Now might be a good time to go back and get the *Griffin*."

The five glanced at one another, then turned and headed to the *Flossy*.

"I think I've had about all the excitement I can stand for one morning," Pete's sister said. "How about dropping me off at the Elliot dock on your way to the sailboat?"

Pete and Dan pushed the *Flossy* off the beach and everyone boarded from the dock.

"I don't know what we'd have done if you hadn't come looking for us," Kate told Cara as the *Flossy* headed out.

"I know what we'd have done," Dan said. "We'd have taken a one-way swim to the bottom of Lake Huron."

"That's right, Cara," Pete added. "Fats would have blown the *Griffin* and us to bits."

"We owe you one, Cara," Eddie chimed in, grinning. "Your next Charleston Chew is on me."

"I may take you up on that, Eddie," Cara replied. "Now, just drop me off at the Elliot, and I'll see if I can't find my way home from there."

Dan pulled the *Flossy* alongside the hotel pier and Cara climbed a boarding ladder up to the dock.

"Thank you so very much," Cara said looking down at her brother with a twinkle of sarcasm. "You know something, Petey-wetey? If mom and dad ever let you off the front porch again in your life, you'll owe it all to my benevolent, short memory."

"Thanks, Cara," Pete said ignoring the taunt. "You can start forgetting right now." He pulled the cord and started toward Middle Entrance.

When Pete drew the *Flossy* alongside the sailboat, Eddie and Dan hopped aboard. Kate sat with Pete as Dan cleated the tow line to the bow of the *Griffin*. The two boats plodded slowly through Middle Entrance and back into Muscallonge Bay.

At Reif's Point, Kate reached out and held Pete's hand. "My family will be going back to Cincinnati pretty soon. We won't see each other again until next year. I want you to know that I'll miss you. Please don't forget me, Pete."

At that, she leaned over and kissed him on the cheek. Her lips were soft and moist and she held his hand in hers. Pete glanced down and gulped nervously as she looked into his eyes. *Forget her? Not likely.*

"If it weren't for you, I would have been killed," she said. Pete's face flushed instantly. He glanced back to the *Griffin* and was relieved to see that both Dan and Eddie were asleep at their stations.

Pete brought the *Griffin* close to the red double-boathouse and Kate called back to awaken her crew. Dan and Eddie sat up and Dan snapped the hook to the mooring ball.

The four exhausted sailors sat in the *Flossy* and Pete guided her from the *Griffin* to the dock. They noticed first Dr. and Mrs. Hinken walking along the path to the boathouse. Behind them were two men wearing the dark blue uniforms of the Michigan State Police with Harold Geetings between them wearing some of Dr. Hinken's clothes and a set of the policeman's handcuffs.

"Oh, children," Mrs. Hinken said, "we had no idea what you had been through. When Mr. Geetings came to, he told us about the murder and the counterfeit money scheme. Then he asked us to telephone the police."

177

"There'll be more officers arriving soon to look for Mr. FitzRoberts," the first trooper said, "but we'll need to take some preliminary statements from each of you. We might as well get comfortable. Where do you recommend?"

"The back room of the Bon Air," Eddie suggested. "I'm about ready for a Jersey Mud."

Dr. Hinken stepped forward. "That sounds like a fine idea, Eddie. This has been a pretty extraordinary day. Suppose we send the *Polly Ann* over and invite the Jenkins to join us. My treat."

"Jersey Mud, eh?" Pete said furrowing his eyebrows in mock deliberation. "Well, okay," he smiled. "What's the chances of Mr. Geetings joining us?"

"Right," Kate agreed. "None of us would be making any statements at all if Mr. Geetings hadn't thrown Fats off his balance at Bosely. He had nothing to gain and everything to lose."

Pete smiled at the old writer. "I'll go to the Bon Air, if we all can go—and we agree to meet there again when Mr. Geetings returns to the Snows. Unless I miss my guess, he'll be back one day with a book about us and our Mackinac passage."

Acknowledgments

Mackinac Passage could not have been completed without the support of friends and relatives who contributed their talents in a variety of ways.

First, foremost, and forever is my family: Candy, my wife, and my four sons, Geoff, Ian, Jamie, and Bo who assisted by reading troublesome chapters and making significant observations and suggestions. My three sisters, Pat, Amy Lou, and Karen advised me in the historical accuracy and incidental facts of the Les Cheneaux Islands. Also Amy Lou lent her proofreading talents and Karen contributed vastly to the worth of the book with her sketches that are found on the cover and at the beginning of each chapter.

Charles Ferry and Peter Sieruta, authors of many young adult novels, provided encouragement and invaluable direction early on in the project. Cammie Mannino, Rochester children's bookstore owner, and Nancy Bujold, youth services director of the Rochester Hills Public Library, furnished insight to the vagaries of young adult literature.

Rochester teachers Ray Lawson and Brian Seyburn, as well as Romulus teachers, George and Danna Bowersox, contributed pails of red ink to the final drafts. Noted literary advisor, Helen Williams, having read an early draft, insisted that I persevere assuring me that the story was worthy of the work needed for its completion.

Close friends Fred Wiseman, Ken Johnson, Dave Barnwell, and Dave Shellenbarger each assisted with their particular qualifications.

For his insight into Great Lakes shipping lore, I give special thanks to a vast wealth of information that I will sorely miss, Great Lakes ore boat captain, Melvin Edwards, who passed away shortly before this book's completion.

Ron and Mary Dufina, longtime friends and residents of Mackinac Island, assisted by checking historical, cultural, and physical facts pertaining to our beloved island.

Unbeknownst to Garrison Keillor, it was the storytelling segment in his weekly *A Prairie Home Companion* radio show that planted the seed for me to begin this project.

Finally, my deepest appreciation goes to my childhood friends, Dan Heekin and Eddie Terrill who, along with their families, remain summer residents in the Snows. Although most of this story is fiction, some is not. I owe them greatly for allowing me to submit to the world, under the veneer-thin guise of fiction, the real life adventures of their youth.